PRAISE FOR

MW01006172

Here are some of the over 100,000 five star reviews left for the Dead Cold Mystery series.

"Rex Stout and Michael Connelly have spawned a protege."

AMAZON REVIEW

"So begins one damned fine read."

AMAZON REVIEW

"Mystery that's more brain than brawn."

AMAZON REVIEW

"I read so many of this genre...and ever so often I strike gold!"

AMAZON REVIEW

"This book is filled with action, intrigue, espionage, and everything else lovers of a good thriller want."

AMAZON REVIEW

A CHRISTMAS KILLING

A DEAD COLD MYSTERY

BLAKE BANNER

RIGHTHOUSE

ISBN-13: 978-1-63696-021-0

ISBN-10: 1-63696-021-9

Cover design by: Damonza

Printed in the United States of America

www.righthouse.com

www.instagram.com/righthousebooks

www.facebook.com/righthousebooks

twitter.com/righthousebooks

DEAD COLD MYSTERY SERIES

ONE

"Lilith was a bit dumb. Her father thought she was smart, but I always thought she was kind of dumb. I know, maybe a mother shouldn't talk like that about her daughter, but what can I tell you but the truth? She wasn't mentally retarded, or like some kids you see who walk around with their mouths open all the time. You know the kind of thing? She wasn't like that. She was bright and fun and always laughing and . . ."

Lilith's mother paused to shake her head and suppress a sob. I watched a tear creep along her lower eyelid and pause before spilling down her cheek toward the corner of her mouth. The Christmas tree in the corner twinkled sadly.

"Affectionate," she said at last and nodded, like she'd chosen a particularly good word. "She was real affectionate with everyone. She was also a bit narcissistic. She hid it because she was so sweet and everybody loved her. But if ever you had a conversation *with* Lilith, the conversation was *about* Lilith." I drew breath to ask a question, but she waved it away like an annoying fly. "You could start a conversation about anything. Before thirty seconds were up, she'd say, 'For *me* . . .' and turn it around so you were talking about her."

Dehan cleared her throat. "We are particularly interested in . . ."

Lilith's mother spoke on. "My mother died. Lilith never knew my mother. She cried nonstop for a week, about the fact that I never let her meet her grandmother. In the end everyone was saying, 'Poor Lilith. She never knew her grandmother. Now she's dead. It must be so hard for her.' I just lost my mother, but screw me." She sighed. "But sweet. Sweet as a sugarplum."

Her eyes strayed to a plum cake that was sitting on a side table, fenced in by sprigs of holly. I said, "So she had a lot of friends?"

"Oh, plenty. Everyone at her job adored her. She was training to be a nurse, you know, but volunteered at a thrift store. You know how it is, Detective Stone, when you look like a Playboy pinup and have the personality of a dumb blonde, you've got a hundred and one friends, and they're all guys who want to get inside your panties. But *are* they friends?"

She spread her hands and nodded slowly, using her whole body. It was meant to be an expression of worldly wisdom. Instead it made her look like a seagull doing a balancing act on a buoy in rough seas.

"Do any of those friends stand out?"

"*All* of them stand out—for the lascivious hypocrites that they were. When they wanted to screw her, they were lining up like dildos on parade! But when she was being killed, where were they?"

Dehan leaned forward with narrowed eyes. "That," she said, "is what we are trying to find out. So what we need to know is, who?"

"Who?"

"Who?" Dehan nodded elaborately, and I couldn't resist asking, "Who?"

She ignored me and spoke to Lilith's mother. "Mrs. Jones, right now, those hundreds of lined-up dildos are just an anonymous mass of latex." Mrs. Jones frowned at the image. Dehan went on regardless. "That doesn't help us. We need a lot more than just general, anonymous latex."

"More than latex?"

"More information. We need to know how many men were lining up for Lilith's favors, we need to know their names and addresses . . ."

Mrs. Jones shrugged. "I don't know . . ."

Dehan reached out her hand and gripped Mrs. Jones' wrist. "That's okay. But think for a moment—wasn't there one who stood out from the rest? Wasn't there one who was a little more keen, called her more often, tried harder than the others . . . ?"

"You mean like a boyfriend?"

Dehan nodded. "For example."

"Well, she *had* a boyfriend."

Dehan sighed. There was a hint of a groan in the sigh. "You didn't mention this in the original police investigation?"

"I was extremely upset. So I don't honestly know *what* I told that detective. He was *fat* and I did not like talking to him. Also, I never met her boyfriend."

I frowned and scratched my chin at the same time. "You never met her boyfriend?"

The coal glowed in the grate, and outside the wind rattled the window and threatened snow. The tinsel on the tree shivered. Mrs. Jones shook her head, and for a moment I thought that was all the answer I was going to get. But finally she said, "Lilith was a strange girl. To anyone who met her she was an angel, sweet, always laughing and kind and gentle. But at home she could be . . ." She nodded several times before saying, ". . . *cutting*."

Dehan echoed her, "Cutting . . ."

"Cutting, like a knife. She told me she didn't want her boyfriend to meet me because I was weird. Weird, me. I have worked my fingers to the bone to put a roof over her head and a plate of food on the table, because her father, may he rot in hell, died on us when she was no more than two years old. Can you believe that? Dying like that? And she says I am *weird*!"

Dehan smiled with her mouth. Her eyes said something that was not infused with the Christmas spirit. "So what *do* you know about her boyfriend, aside from the fact that she had one?"

"Uh . . . nothing?"

Dehan turned to me with a face like a summons. I gave my head a small, one-sided shake and drew breath to speak to Mrs. Jones. She preempted me.

"Then there was Ern."

"Ern?"

"Ern was Pat's brother. I told your fat detective about him. He's fat too, like Pat. They were all fat. They would have been good friends, getting fat together."

"About Ern and Lilith . . . ?"

"He was obsessed with her: O-B-S-E-S-T! When he came to visit Pat and Cyril, which was often, he could never stay in his sister's house. He just *had* to come over here and start sniffing around Lilith's skirts."

I glanced at Dehan. She gave a fractional shrug. Brother Ernest had been mentioned in Mo's report, but nothing about his obsession with Lilith. I allowed my eyebrows to say I was interested and asked her, "What do you mean exactly by the phrase, 'sniffing around her skirts'?"

Mrs. Jones looked at Dehan and smiled maliciously. "That's cute," she said. "A homicide cop in the Bronx who has managed to hold on to his innocence."

Dehan's smile was dangerous. "Oh, I think he knows what the expression means, Mrs. Jones, but I think my partner would like to know what Ern used to do. What was his behavior? What makes you say that he was 'sniffing around her skirts.' Precisely, what did he do?"

"I would offer you eggnog, but I am keeping it for my family when they come and visit."

"Thanks, we're on duty. His behavior?"

"He's a mental retard. He's smart enough to tie his shoes and do a simple job. I don't know what he does, but it's simple, you can be sure of that." Her lip curled into an unpleasant smile. "Maybe he's a janitor or something. Anyhow, he used to come 'round and sit where you're sitting"—she pointed at me—"and just kind of gawp at Lilith, and ask her stupid questions . . ."

Dehan asked, "What kind of questions?"

Mrs. Jones sighed. "Like, did she have a boyfriend, was she ever going to get married, would she go to the cinema with him. Once he asked her if she would marry him, another time he asked her what color her panties were. That time I got mad and threw him out. After that he used to come and stand at the fence looking in, and Lilith felt sorry for him—or loved the attention, take your pick—and she'd go and stand talking to him over the fence. So I had to let him come in again."

I nodded and cleared my throat. "So, was he here that Christmas Eve when Lilith was murdered?"

"Yup."

I waited. She watched me wait. Dehan said, "You want to tell us about that?"

She shrugged. "What do you want me to tell you? I already told the detective the first time he came 'round, a year ago. Ern came 'round Christmas morning. He wanted to show us some stupid sweater and socks he'd got from his sister and her husband. The sweater was big, fat horizontal red-and-white stripes with reindeer and stupid stuff like that on it. All the noses and the antlers were in relief, you know the kind of thing. The socks matched the sweater. They were both nauseating, but like I said, he was kind of stupid and he liked them, and he wanted to show Lilith."

"What sort of time was that?"

"Just around the time you're most busy in the kitchen preparing the Christmas dinner, about ten or eleven in the morning. He turns up at the door looking more like something out of Halloween than Christmas morning, with that goofy face, saying, 'Hellow, Mrs. Jones, is Lilith in? I want to show her my pwesents.' I called her, I said, 'Lilith, it's your boyfriend!'

You should have seen his face. It was redder than his damn sweater."

Dehan smiled. "You were making Christmas dinner for you and Lilith? Nobody else?"

"Just me and her. There was nobody else. I told her to bring her boyfriend for Christmas, to meet her mom. But she told me, 'No, I don't want him to meet you, Mom, because you're weird.' Weird, me. Me, weird. I ask you directly, Detective Stone, do I look weird to you?"

Aside from her peroxide hair and her very red lips, she did not look especially weird, but it was a conversation I was not keen to get into. I gave her a sympathetic smile instead and asked her, "So it was just the two of you for Christmas dinner, and then Ern showed up. What happened next?"

"What happened next? Well she sat with him in the parlor while he drooled over her and I roasted a turkey, made stuffing, prepared more eggnog . . ."

"That's rough." Dehan shook her head. "I hate it when that happens. What happened after that?"

"Well, then Cyril came over to get Ern."

"Cyril was Ern's brother-in-law."

"Still is, far as I know. Little mincing mouse of a man. Humble. You know the sort. I don't hate him. He's a nice man, always polite, always helpful, but so damn humble sometimes I just want to backhand him and tell him to man up. You just don't get real men anymore, Detective Stone. My Davie, now that was a man. No BS, one hundred percent testosterone-fueled man. Now he's dead, the son of a bitch. But I see men today, with their moisturizing creams, their hair conditioners, and their pink shirts, and I fear for the future of our race. Don't you?"

"All the time. So he came over to collect Ern, and then what happened?"

She rolled her eyes and gave her peroxide hair a shake. I looked at the angel on the top of the tree, and it struck me there was something manic about the way she was staring at the ceiling.

"Well, Lilith, who just couldn't get enough male attention, started offering them eggnog and fruitcake and this and that, and I'm saying to her, 'Well, come on, honey, they have to get back and help with *their own* Christmas dinner!' Kind of hinting discreetly, but when Lilith was lapping up attention, you couldn't get through to her. She was just: 'Oh, Mom! Cyril and Ern just popped over in the spirit of the season to say hi. Least we can do is show some hospitality!' So they stayed, and we were getting closer and closer to lunchtime and I just did not know what to do!"

"Okay, stop."

She stared at me wide-eyed. Dehan arched an eyebrow at me. I raised one hand and said, "I need to be clear about this. Cyril joined Ern here and Lilith encouraged them both to stay."

"That *is* what I just said."

"Okay, let's take this one step at a time. How did Ern react to Cyril's arrival?"

"Well he didn't break open the champagne, if that's what you mean. Cyril is smart and funny. He won't prepossess you with his appearance, but he's smart and he has a real funny sense of humor. He's shy, when there's lots of people, like, but when it's just a few friends he comes out of his shell and he is real funny. So when he showed up and started stealing the scene, Ern wasn't too happy."

Dehan spoke my thoughts. "How did that manifest? What did he do?"

She shrugged. "He sulked. He sat right there on the sofa with his hands in his lap and his big fat bottom lip stuck out and stared at his knees."

"While Cyril sat and made Lilith laugh?"

"And I worked my pretty little butt off in the kitchen."

Dehan suppressed a sigh by tying her hair in a knot at the back of her neck, narrowed her eyes, and asked, "How did you get them to leave?"

"I didn't. Like I told your fat detective, I couldn't get them to leave. It was two thirty before they went. And they only went because the big battleship came and got them."

"The big battleship?"

"Patricia, Cyril's wife, Ern's sister. She looked like a Spanish galleon in full sail. She came down my path like eight sacks of angry jelly and started pounding on my door. 'Cyril Perkins! Are you in there? You come out here right this minute!' Well you should have seen Ern jump. Cyril apologized for staying so long, and Lilith saw them to the door. I came out following, wiping my hands on a tea towel."

She put her fingertips to her forehead and gave a small shake.

"I have never . . . in my life . . . *seen* such a spectacle. You would not credit it if you did not see it. She was *howling* like a dog, waving her great arms about, wobbling like three hundred pounds of aspic, and the *language*! Well, as my sainted grandmother used to say, 'I do declare! Them words would make the Devil himself blush!'"

"What," said Dehan, and narrowed her eyes again. "What was it, exactly, that she was mad about?"

"The most ridiculous thing I ever heard. She thought that Cyril and Lilith were having an affair!"

"What made her think that?"

"Blessed if I know! Lilith was very sociable, very friendly, and very affectionate, and as I may have pointed out earlier, she was a sucker for male attention. Often when she came home from work, Cyril would be in his front yard smoking his pipe and they would stop and talk. Other times she would invite him over for afternoon coffee and they'd sit and talk. He always made her laugh a lot. But he is just a timid old man with a lively sense of humor. Pat was insane to think there was anything going on. A beautiful young girl like her and an old man like him. Why, he must be sixty, and at that time, last year, she was just twenty-three. The idea is just disgusting."

I scratched my chin. "Any idea what put it in her head?"

"Sure. She's crazy. She's fat, ugly, and stupid and spends her whole day imagining her husband is out doing the kinds of things she wishes she was doing."

I grunted. Pop psychology I could come up with myself. What I needed was facts—the facts Mo had missed a year back when he took the case.

"Anything more concrete than that?"

She shook her head. "No. It was based on nothing. I mean, the man watched Lilith grow up, for heaven's sake. And as she got older, they became garden fence friends. But Pat was such a bitter, twisted, evil woman that she read wickedness into everything." She paused a moment, suddenly serious and thoughtful. "I think it had a lot more to do with Lilith and Pat than it had to do with Cyril. Lilith was young and beautiful, Pat was grotesque, and she knew she was getting old. She just hated Lilith, plain and simple."

Dehan nodded, like it made sense to her. "Did anything she say, any phrase or word, strike you as especially significant?"

"No, she said she, Lilith, was well named, called her a whore, a thief, stealing other women's husbands, a tramp, a cheap slut . . ." She shrugged, then smiled at Dehan. "Lilith was vain, a narcissist, but she didn't deserve to be called those things. She was a nice kid, a good girl."

And then the tears started to spill again, slipping down her cheeks, touched with fire and the colored sparkles of Christmas.

Mrs. Jones rose and went to the kitchen. She returned a couple of minutes later with a tray of coffee and a glass of eggnog for herself. She set them down and sat. The room was very quiet. She was gazing into her drink, biting her lip and tipping her head from side to side, as though she had found something infinitely sad in her glass of eggnog.

After a moment she gave an extremely heavy sigh and spoke.

"Cyril and Ern managed to pull her back down the road. It wasn't easy. There had been a bit of snow and the sidewalk was slippery, and she was big and struggling and screaming. I remember a few of the neighbors had come out to see what all the ruckus was about. She just ignored them and kept turning back and shouting abuse at Lilith, telling her to keep her filthy hands to herself, until they got to their house. They pushed her through the gate and up the steps and that was the last we saw of them . . . At least it was the last I saw of them."

Dehan's voice was quiet. "What do you mean by that, Mrs. Jones?"

Mrs. Jones raised her eyes to look at Dehan's face. They were full of reproach, anger, and incomprehension. "Well, Lilith saw Pat again, didn't she? Later that evening. I sent her, like I did every year, to take a Christmas supper to old Mrs. Rodriguez down on the corner of Gildersleeve. Some turkey, mashed potatoes, broccoli, Christmas pudding . . ."

She trailed off, staring at us each in turn. I waited. She spoke suddenly, and her voice was startling and loud.

"She's dead now. Mrs. Rodriguez. She was very old. She died March fourth. That was the last Christmas meal I ever sent her. Lilith went over at like four in the afternoon, and she stayed with her till about seven I guess. I don't know what time, really, but at least seven. She was good like that, kind, you know? Affectionate. So when she came back it was dark. All the windows down Pugsley Avenue had their drapes closed. All the doors were closed. Everybody was watching a movie, sleeping in front of the fire after Christmas lunch, stroking the cat, or the dogs . . ."

Her eyes were wide and unseeing, staring at the window where already the early-afternoon light was beginning to fade. She blinked and looked down at the floor. "She had dogs," she said. "Pat, two nasty little ratlike dogs, always yapping. By seven thirty I was getting worried, so just before eight I called Mrs. Rodriguez and asked to speak with Lilith. She said Lilith had gone about half an hour earlier. So I thought, maybe she'd fallen and hurt herself . . ."

The flood came again, harder this time. Her eyes were bright but glazed with tears, her nose suddenly red, as though from a cold. Her bottom lip curled in under her teeth, and she pulled a handkerchief from her cardigan pocket to cover her mouth and hide her grief.

"If only . . ." The words came out ugly and twisted with grief. "If only she had fallen . . ."

She hunched forward, pushing her elbows into her belly, pressing the handkerchief over her mouth, her shoulders shaking convulsively, but in complete silence, until her voice broke free and she cried, "*Oh God! Oh God, dear Lord, if only she had fallen . . .!*"

Dehan rose and sat next to her, encircled her with her arms, and held her until the storm subsided. Mrs. Jones blew her nose and wiped streaks of wet mascara across her cheeks.

"I found her. She was lying on her face, with her legs slightly apart. It looked so strange, like she was just having a little rest. She had her coat open. I remember thinking she'd catch cold. And then I saw the big stain. We only have one streetlamp on Pugsley Avenue, and it was across from where she was lying, but it was enough to see the blood. She'd been stabbed with a big pair of scissors, right in the middle of her back. There was lots of . . . lots of blood. And when I looked at her face, her eyes were open, just looking across the sidewalk at the wall. She looked surprised, more than anything else."

She unfolded her handkerchief and examined it for a while, as though it really was interesting. When she spoke again, she was frowning at the handkerchief. "She was lying right outside Pat and Cyril's house, just past their gate."

TWO

WE STEPPED OUT INTO THE FROSTED STREET. THE trees, naked and cold, reached twiggy fingers toward an unfriendly, gunmetal-gray sky, weighed low with sagging clouds. The roofs of the odd jumble of houses that was Pugsley Avenue were lightly dusted with snow, and small drifts had accumulated beside chimney pots, against garden walls and car tires.

Dehan shuddered beside me as she looked up at the bellying menace of the clouds and pulled her coat close about her throat. She had on a woolly hat with a pom-pom, and I noted that her cheeks and the tip of her nose had turned pink, but I made no comment.

It was no more than thirty yards from Mrs. Jones' house to Cyril Perkins' house. To our left a road sign reading *END* stood before a wall of trees that was the southernmost end of Pugsley Creek Park. We stepped onto the icy blacktop and walked with care. There was no sidewalk at that section of the avenue, and the road surface was slippery with black ice.

Cyril Perkins' house was an ugly, three-story gabled affair in beige stone. A flight of nine steps formed a dogleg up to a porch that sat above a narrow basement window. We climbed the cold, concrete steps, and Dehan rang the bell while she stamped her feet, then breathed condensation into her woolen gloves. When he didn't open straightaway, she rapped on the wood with her knuckles, and a small voice came from inside, saying the owner was coming.

The door opened a moment later to reveal a small man with amused blue eyes. He had thin hair on a round head, reading glasses suspended on a chain around his neck, and a cardigan that had become lost somewhere between green and beige sometime in the early 1950s. His plaid, fur-lined slippers said he was not going to be taking swift action over anything anytime soon. There was a sweet aroma of pipe tobacco lingering on the air.

I showed him my badge, and Dehan fumbled hers out of her pocket with woolen fingers.

"Good afternoon, I am Detective John Stone of the NYPD, this is Detective Dehan. May we have a word with you about your wife, Patricia Perkins?"

His eyes went wide, and his eyebrows rose up his forehead. I thought he looked worried. "Have you found her? Is she all right?"

Dehan answered. "No, Mr. Perkins, we haven't found her yet. But it is *very* cold out here . . ."

He blinked once, then stood back, pulling the door open with him. "Of course! Of course! Please, come into the parlor where it is warm. I have a fire burning. It is a wicked day. Will you have some coffee?"

"Yes!" It was Dehan. She glanced at me as we stepped through the door into the living room and added, "Please. That would be nice."

What he called the parlor was a large, long room with two windows overlooking a backyard with a vegetable patch and tall trees that towered over the house. The drapes were half-drawn, to allow in light but keep out the cold. To the left a dark dining table stood on a dark, wooden floor, and beyond it a door gave on to a kitchen that had been modern 'round about the time his cardigan was knitted.

To the right there was a large fireplace where he had logs burning over smokeless coals. The walls were a dull cream with large, framed prints of famous Impressionist paintings. An ancient, heavy, three-piece suite in dark green was ranged around the fire. His chair was easily identified by the occasional table beside it that held a cup, a book by Steinbeck, and an old ashtray with a pipe sitting in it.

He paused in the middle of the floor, took our coats, and gestured at the suite with both hands.

"Please, sit. I will be but a couple of minutes. Make yourselves comfortable and, above all, warm!"

I went and lowered myself into an armchair while Dehan leaned over the fireplace, warming her hands while the orange light bathed her face. After a while she stood with her back to the flames and mouthed at me, *No Christmas decorations!*

I made a face that said maybe he'd lost his taste for that kind of thing. That can happen when your wife kills your neighbor with a pair of scissors on Christmas Day.

She cocked her head and made a kind of shrug with her head that said maybe I had a point at that.

Cyril Perkins came out of the kitchen with a green wooden tray laden with coffee, cream, sugar, and Christmas pudding. He settled himself in his chair, set the tray on the table with an air of satisfaction, and set about pouring the coffee and sharing it out, like Santa handing out presents. As he served the pudding and handed it to Dehan, he said, "So you are not here to tell me you have found Pat."

Dehan helped herself to cream in her coffee and on the pudding and stuffed a surprising amount into her mouth. After that she said, "M'fwaid nodg, Mshta Pwkinsh."

I nodded and smiled at her and said, "I'm afraid not, Mr. Perkins. I head up a cold-cases unit at the Forty-Third, and though this case is only a year old . . ."

His eyebrows shot up, and he pierced me with very bright blue eyes. "Only?"

I nodded. "Forgive my choice of words. Working homicide can make you a little callous at times. I assure you we take every case extremely seriously. My partner and I have worked cases that were twenty and thirty years old. As cold cases go, one year is comparatively recent. For you, of course, it is quite different."

He seemed to study my face for a moment, blinked a couple of times, and returned to his coffee. "I understand that," he said, "but it has been a very long year." He sipped. "So the case has gone cold, and it has been passed to you."

"Yes. We have all the background, we have the reports from the ME and the investigating team at the time . . ." I tasted the pudding. It was extremely good. I sipped the coffee. It was also extremely good. As I set down the cup I said, "But as a methodology it seems to me unwise to start your investigation on the same foundations of a prior investigation which failed to produce results."

He wiped his mouth on a paper napkin and smiled warmly at me. "One is led to believe that the police, or the cops, should I say, are hard-boiled, unimaginative, and lacking in human depth. But your thinking is almost philosophical. That is good. So you, Detective Stone, like to go right back to the beginning and look at everything with fresh eyes. The evidence—or what is left of it—has not changed, but the perception of the investigator has. So, what would you like to know?"

Dehan struggled to swallow, but I beat her to the question. "What was it about Lilith that Pat hated so much?"

He set down his cup and saucer with great care and dabbed at his lips again.

"It is perception again, isn't it? I don't believe she hated Lilith, I believe she hated herself and projected her hatred onto Lilith, because Lilith was everything that she wanted to be and felt unable to become. She didn't know, or didn't care, that I loved her for what she was. It wasn't . . ." He wrinkled his eyes in a smile. "As people are so fond of saying these days, it wasn't *about* me. Pat was the issue: her self-loathing, her anger, her inability to rise above the limitations of her appetites and her fat, her unrelenting belief that problems could be solved instantly, at the stroke of an angry phone call, a fit of rage . . . or a pair of scissors."

All trace of his earlier smile had faded to an expression of infinite sadness. "I had no desire for her to be like Lilith. Lilith would have bored me to distraction, charming and beautiful as she was. But the tragedy was that Pat had never really loved me, or anyone else for that matter. Pat saw the world as a place where she had to impose her ego at all costs. It was as though her very survival depended on it. I was no more than another possession which she used or deployed at will in the service of her own self-aggrandizement. She was the queen, the empress, of the universe, and any who crossed her or defied her were dealt with in no uncertain terms."

Dehan had stopped eating and drinking and had been watching him carefully. Now she cleared her throat and arched an eyebrow at him.

"I'm a little confused . . ."

He laughed with genuine amusement and leaned back in his chair. "I am not surprised, Detective Dehan!"

She didn't pause. "You claim that you loved her as she was and that you didn't want her to change, and yet you describe her as . . ."

For a moment she was lost for words and shrugged. He said, "An abominable woman."

She nodded. "Yes, really. I mean, you make her sound awful." She shook her head and shrugged. "So what was to love?"

He sighed, not with impatience, but with the effort of putting into words something which was inexplicable. Eventually he said, "Are you familiar with Iris Murdoch, Detective Dehan?"

"I know the name . . ."

"She was one of the great writers of the twentieth century, a real intellectual, a Buddhist, an existentialist, deeply in love with Jean-Paul . . ." He smiled, closed his eyes, and shook his head. "I digress. I could hear Pat right then: 'Here we go, sit down, ladies and gentlemen, for the great lecture!'"

He picked up his pipe, examined it a moment, and set it down again. "In *The Sea, The Sea*, she writes a fascinating portrait of a man who is incapable of understanding the relationship between the woman he loves and her husband. And the point is that what connects people is not what they like about each other. It is the needs they satisfy in each other that bind them. And Pat, for all her ill humor, her egotism, and occasional cruelty, satisfied deep needs in me. Detective, I have no shame in admitting that she gave me security. She made me feel safe, and I miss her every day. Every night I pray that she will come back to me, and that we will be able to prove her innocence in this appalling affair." He glanced at Dehan and laughed out loud at the expression on her face. "Love," he said, "is no more than need, Detective Dehan. Love is just need."

I sipped my coffee and set down the cup. "That is a little beyond our remit . . ."

"And yet it is at the heart of every motive for murder since people started murdering each other."

"You're probably right, Mr. Perkins, but I'm afraid we need to stick with concrete facts. Could you outline for us, please, the events of that day? I believe you had your wife's brother staying with you . . ."

He gave a small grunt and nodded. "Ernest, or as he is popularly known, Ern. Yes, Pat insisted he should be there every Christmas. It was not so much a case of being charitable to him—I am quite sure he could have had much nicer Christmases than he enjoyed with us—it was more a case of exercising control over him, or perhaps more to the point, of having a group of dependent people gathered around her, praising her and receiving her bounty."

I said, "You're pretty scathing about her, Mr. Perkins."

He chuckled. "Don't read too much into that, Detective Stone. I am sarcastic by nature. I had a reputation for it among the boys, and my fellow teachers were well aware of it. They used to call me Ascorbic Cyril." He shrugged and gave his head a little shake. "I can't pretend that I liked Pat. There was very little to like. But I did love her very dearly. She fulfilled me somehow, and as I said, I pray nightly for her return."

Dehan broke in, "Okay, so Ern was here. Was there anybody else?"

"No, just the three of us."

"And what was the deal with Ern and Lilith?"

"The deal . . ."

He gazed into the flames, absently picked up his pipe, and started to fill it with a strong, sweet tobacco. He took his time lighting it with two long tapers, which he shook out and tossed into the hot embers.

"Not to put too fine a point on it, Detective Dehan, Ern was obsessed with Lilith. Of course we and the Joneses have been neighbors for years, and we had watched Lilith grow from a baby into a fine young lady. Her mother was, and indeed is, somewhat peculiar, but she was a very good mother and raised a very lovely daughter. You may not think so to look at me, Detectives, but I have a gift with children. I have worked with children all my adult life, and for some reason they seem to like me. Lilith was no different. Gwen—that's Mrs. Jones—and I would often stop for a chat, especially after her husband died, and little Lilith would always be with her, naturally, and as the child began to grow and develop intellectually, we developed the kind of friendship that grows between a child and a favored uncle."

"Did you visit with them?"

"No." He shook his head firmly. "No, not at first, but when Lilith was about ten, and it began to become clear that Gwen would probably remain single, they both began to invite me over occasionally for tea and cakes, and that sort of thing. I think it was nice for Gwen to have a male figure around, albeit an uncleish one, to help out with a few small things like changing a plug or writing a stern letter to the bank."

He gave a small, self-deprecating smile.

"Not surprisingly, Pat was not very amused by my occasional visits to the Joneses' house. At first she did little more than grumble, as the invites tended to take the form of a request for help followed by an offer of coffee and chocolate brownies. But as we became more familiar, closer, the invites themselves also became more relaxed in nature. It might be that Lilith had a presentation at school: Would I like to watch her dress rehearsal? Or celebrate the fact that it had gone well!

"When the nature of the invites changed, then Pat began to resent them more. That was when she started to insist on Ern visiting us on a regular basis, and once he was here, she would find every conceivable pretext to send him over to the Joneses'. It might be to borrow a cup of sugar, to *return* a pound of sugar . . ."

Dehan was frowning, scratching her shiny black head. "What was the purpose of sending Ern over . . ."

He smiled, then gave a small laugh. "Well, primarily to sabotage any intimate friendship that might be developing between Gwen and myself, but also in the hope that, as Lilith began to develop as a young woman, Ern would fall in love with her."

"She *wanted* Ern to fall in love with Lilith?"

"Oh, certainly!" He laughed. "That way Pat could cause extreme discomfort to Gwen and Lilith, make my presence undesirable by association, and guarantee herself an excuse to go barging over there anytime she wanted to and burst in on whatever she imagined was happening."

I said, "And that was, in fact, what happened on that Christmas Day."

He seemed not to hear and went on, speaking softly. "The thing was, Ern did in fact become obsessed with Lilith. He was . . ." He sucked in his lips and shook his head at the fire. "We are so precious these days, so afraid of offending, that we have forgotten often it is the truth that offends. The Spanish call them subnormal; we used to call them mentally retarded. Today we have to say that they have learning difficulties. But the fact remains that a rose by any other name is the same flower. However precious and anally retentive we care to be, Ern was both subnormal and mentally retarded. He was simple and had the mentality of a five-year-old child. It was a congenital condition. Both of their parents were mental retards. When I tell you that Pat was the intelligent one in the family, you will get some idea of what they were like."

Dehan was frowning hard. "So, does Pat have mental health issues?"

He puffed at his pipe, watching her for a moment. "Mental health issues? Another one of those sanitized, modern expressions. Her IQ was bang on one hundred. What most people don't realize is that one hundred, the average, is not even bright. It is dull, unimaginative, simple. And that was her. She had a certain low cunning about her, but she was not bright. She saw things in black-and-white terms of what was right or wrong according to her principles, and her principles were mainly shaped by what she wanted or didn't want.

"Whether she was in any way traumatized by her parents, I am not sure. Whether she was neurotic, I am not sure. She was certainly not psychotic. I think she was quite simply greedy and not very bright."

"That's another pretty harsh assessment, Mr. Perkins."

"Is it? Life is harsh. Reality is harsh, Detective Stone. She was born of mentally retarded parents and had a mentally retarded brother; it was a miracle she was not herself a mental retard. She had the good fortune to meet a man who loved her, who was able to value and treasure those aspects of her personality which were beautiful and valuable."

Dehan raised an eyebrow. "What are those aspects? We haven't heard anything about them yet."

He answered without hesitation. "She was a wonderful, loving mother. She was . . ." He thought a moment, then laughed. "She was *abundant*, generous, giving, like a primal force of nature. When she was not angry, she was delightful. She was strong, uncompromising, pure, and raw. I have an IQ of one hundred and fifty-five, Detectives, and she would often shake her head and say, 'I don't know what you see in me, Cyril,' and I would tell her that was because she was simple, and we would both laugh. I could never explain to her why I loved her, nor did she really want to know. It was enough that I did love her. But for me it was a fascination—an intoxication—with those primal forces that were so powerfully abundant in her."

I scratched my chin. "You say she was a wonderful mother . . ."

"Superb."

"You have a daughter, right?"

"Theresa." He smiled. "Fortunately she inherited my brains and the good side of her mother's nature. She is a very talented young doctor at the Harlem Hospital, and much of what she has achieved is down to her mother's diligence and hard work."

We fell silent for a moment. I gazed at the dancing flames and felt momentarily sleepy in the close, warm room.

"Can you tell us what happened that day, Mr. Perkins?"

He nodded several times. "I can tell you exactly what happened that day."

THREE

"THERESA WAS WORKING THAT WEEK. THIS IS THE sacrifice that doctors make. Their life is not their own. It belongs to their patients. Or to the hospital that employs them. But I digress. Pat had insisted once again on having Ern stay with us. He had a small apartment near Hunts Point where he lived a squalid, unhappy, lonely life. I confess that about three hundred and fifty days of the year we paid very little attention to him, and I would happily have ignored him the remaining fifteen days, but Pat had some qua-religious idea that if she was nice to him at Christmas she would somehow qualify as a good person, despite the way she treated him the rest of the year. That was Pat's simplistic way of thinking: the rule is, be kind at Christmas, so that was what she did.

"She had sent me over Christmas Eve in the morning to collect him. I knew from the start that he was going to be a nuisance because he had bought Lilith a whole bag of presents. Mainly they consisted of plastic bead necklaces and bracelets, and cheap perfume from the local drugstore. There were also pictures he had cut out from magazines—pictures of horses, or sunsets, or forests in New England in the fall, you know the sort of thing.

"I advised him that maybe it wasn't such a great idea to overwhelm her with cheap presents, and maybe we could stop at a store and buy her one thing that we could be sure she would like, but he was adamant. These were his treasures for her.

"So, on Christmas morning, after we had given each other our presents under the tree, he bathed, shaved, and dressed and took himself down the road to the Joneses' house. Conversation at home, from that point on, between Pat and myself, was pretty limited. In fact, it was more of a monologue than a dialogue, a monologue in which she ranted about how the Joneses were precious and stuck-up, persnickety and narrow-minded, and how Ern was going to drive them crazy and they would never want to have anything to do with us ever again. She said all this, and repeated it over and over again, with a smug smile on her face. I think you would call that incongruent: her words expressed something regrettable, but her facial demeanor and her tone of voice displayed happiness and satisfaction."

He shrugged, then smiled. "She was, so to speak, weaponizing Ern in order to destroy what shreds of friendship remained between us, as families. However, by midday Ern had not been sent packing. On the contrary, he was still there, eating cake and drinking coffee, and chatting away to Lilith."

Dehan had been watching him through narrowed eyes. Now she reached behind her head and gathered up her abundant black hair, which had untied itself, and tied it into a knot again. As she did it, she said, "So you decided to go and join him?"

He gave his comfortable chuckle again, and his eyes actually seemed to twinkle. "If I am perfectly honest, I went over with the intention of bringing him home for lunch. Pat and I had been busy in the kitchen, but once there the atmosphere was so friendly and agreeable, so very different from the atmosphere I had left behind at my own home, that I allowed myself to be induced to stay."

Dehan arched a withering eyebrow. "Who induced you to stay?"

He didn't miss the implication of the question. "Ahhh . . . I am afraid, flattering as your question is, there was none of that. There are men, like George Clooney, Picasso, Clint Eastwood, who even in their later years retain a magnetic attraction for women. I am not one of those men. Even as a young man, Detective Dehan, women were not attracted to me. I haven't got 'it.' Gwen enjoyed my company and was fond of me, while Lilith and I had a friendship founded on having known each other for many years. I was like an uncle for her. Certainly at her tender years she had no other kind of interest in me." He paused, gazing at Dehan with amused eyes. "So in answer to your question, they both induced me to stay, but only through simple friendship, nothing more."

He paused a moment in thought, gazing at the hypnotic dance of the flames.

"I suppose we lost track of time, Ern indulging his besotted obsession with Lilith, and I enjoying the pleasant atmosphere of a happy home.

"I don't normally drink much, but we had a couple of eggnogs, and before I knew it, it was becoming dusk outside and there was a fearful banging at the door. Pat had come over and was raging. She rang the bell, beat the door, and demanded that Ern and I go outside. Dear Gwen, bless her, urged her to come inside, but the more agreeable Gwen tried to be, the more furious Pat became. Her language, I'm afraid, descended somewhat south of the gutter, and she accused Lilith of things that were quite unwarranted. She used various epithets that made Lilith out to be a prostitute and suggested, quite ridiculously, that Lilith was engaged in an illicit, adulterous relationship with me.

"In the end, between us, Ern and I managed to drag Pat home, and we left Lilith and Gwen to enjoy a quiet, belated Christmas luncheon together. Our own luncheon was not to be enjoyed. Pat was furious. It was hard to pin down exactly what she was furious about, but it seemed that she felt Gwen and Lilith Jones were out to steal her family from her. Her ranting and raving became so extreme and extravagant that Ernest, who is normally oblivious to most things, became quite upset, and no sooner had we finished eating than I packed him in the car and took him, well"—he hesitated a moment—"home."

I asked, "Was that unusual?"

"Oh yes, normally he would have stayed another few days, at least until New Year's, but Pat seemed exceptionally upset, and he was vulnerable. So I thought it wise to remove him from the situation. Besides, Theresa and I had arranged new, more comfortable lodgings for him, at the St. George's Clinic for the Vulnerable and At Risk. Pat knew nothing about it. She would never have approved."

He sat staring at the bowl of his pipe for a moment. His face was suddenly drawn and sallow. "To some extent I blame myself for what happened next. I think I had grown so accustomed to Pat's behavior, her constant complaining and sniping, that I had failed to notice it was getting worse."

He looked up, and I was struck by how direct his gaze was. "Of course I missed the times when we would laugh. She had an extraordinary sense of humor—not sophisticated or subtle, but huge. She would become helpless with laughter on seeing baby ducks staggering after their mother. I remember she was in bed one night, and I was undressing. I was telling her about my day at work, and I told her, 'The kids were fascinated by Uranus,' but I pronounced it the vulgar, popular way, as, 'your anus.' Well, if I said she was helpless with laughter for the next twenty minutes I would not be exaggerating. And for the next week, remembering it was enough to set her off again. She had a vast capacity for laughter." He paused, nodding. "I missed that, because her laughter had dried up, but it is also true that I had failed to read the signs of how bad she felt, how desolate and alone she must have felt."

Dehan said, "What happened?"

"I took Ernest home, told him I might return for him the next day, and drove back to Pat. But when I got home, Pat wasn't there." He puffed out his cheeks, closed his eyes, and blew. "I have been told, your first detective told me, that I walked right past where Lilith was lying. She was just twenty-five feet from where I passed. I have measured it. There is but one lamppost in this section of the avenue, and its light is largely filtered through the foliage of the trees. In December it was dark, clouded, and moonless." He shook his head. "But all the explanations in the world will never rid me of the feeling of horror and regret, that I walked past poor Lilith's body without seeing her.

"The first indication I had that something was wrong was when I realized that Pat's car was gone. It was a big Toyota RAV4; I assumed that she had gone for a drive to cool off. It struck me as odd and, I have to say, extremely out of character, but before I could give it much thought, I had gone inside the house.

"At first I didn't notice anything wrong. Everything seemed to be exactly as I had left it, except that there was an unearthly silence and . . ." He nodded and made a rueful smile. "It slowly dawned on me that the fact that everything was exactly as I had left it was, in itself, wrong. Pat was obsessive. She would have cleared the table, loaded the dishwasher, made coffee. But it was as though she had vanished from the face of the Earth the moment I had stepped outside the door. I checked the whole house and I called her on her cell, but I got no reply, and eventually her cell went dead."

He fell silent. I asked, "What did you do?"

"At first I had no idea *what* to do. It was so out of character! Then it occurred to me that maybe she had gone back to the Joneses' house, to take up with Lilith where she had left off. But the thought had no sooner crossed my mind than I heard those terrible screams. They will live with me for the rest of my life."

"What did you do?"

"I ran!"

"You ran?"

"I ran, out of the house and down the steps. It was dark, and it was sleeting. It was bizarre because for a moment all I could think about was how luminous the specks of sleet were in the darkness, and yet there was that terrible screaming going on. The human mind is strange like that. Then I ran down to the sidewalk and saw Gwen kneeling beside a dark bulk, shaking it and screaming."

He stopped dead, staring sidelong at the flames in the fireplace. We waited in a silence that almost rang in your ears; the crackle and spit of the fire seemed to slide across the face of that silence, without ever disturbing it. When he spoke again it was quite sudden.

"I hurried over. All sorts of crazy thoughts crossed my mind. I wondered if it was a dog that had been run over and wondered at the intensity of Gwen's grief over a dog. I even wondered if it was Pat. What never crossed my mind was that it might be Lilith. That never crossed my mind for a moment. How could anything like that happen? And when I . . ."

He stopped and stared at me. There was outrage in his eyes. He turned his stare on Dehan, as though we had both proposed something insane and offensive.

"When I saw that it was her. I thought . . ." He shook his head. "I thought she'd slipped, tripped, fallen . . . And then I began to see: her eyes were open, she was facedown, staring at the wall, the scissors poking grotesquely, obscenely out of her back, the blood; and you think, maybe it wasn't lethal, maybe she can still be saved. But you can see her eyes are open. And when Gwen shook her, it was horrific, like trying to shake putty . . ."

Dehan said, "You were fond of her."

"Very. Of course. I guess she was like a niece, only, as I had watched her grow up, and we had become friends, it was more than that."

"What happened next?"

"I can't remember who called the police. It may even have been me. My memory becomes very patchy at this point. I know very shortly after that our quiet street was full of flashing red-and-blue lights, and your detective was asking lots of questions about my wife and how she got on with Lilith." He gave a small laugh.

"You don't need to be Sherlock Holmes to see the implications, but"—he shook his head—"I still find it very hard to believe that Pat, for all that she was a very strong, angry woman, that she should be capable of killing. I find that very hard to accept."

I nodded for a few seconds, slowly, sucking my teeth. "The scissors?"

He sighed and screwed up his eyes, pinching the bridge of his nose. "Yes, yes, I know. They were from her sewing set, and they had her prints on them, as they naturally would, being hers!"

Dehan offered a humorless, lopsided smile. "But I think the important point, Mr. Perkins, is that they had nobody else's prints on them." He didn't open his eyes. He just nodded. She went on, "She took her car, and here's the part I am having trouble with, Mr. Perkins: nobody knew her better than you did, but you have no idea where she went. How is that possible?"

He sighed, then opened his eyes and flopped back in his chair.

"I can see how you would think that, but actually you are quite wrong. Did you know that statistically, fat people are more likely to be secretive than thin or normal-weight people?"

"No, I didn't know that."

"Well, it was certainly true of Pat. Everything in her life was on a need-to-know basis, and nobody needed to know anything, except her. She was obsessive about it. She'd tell you they weren't secrets, but that nobody had any business knowing anything about her private life. Sometimes it was stupid things like whether she had bought lamb or chicken for dinner. Other times it was more intimate, private stuff, like not wanting to put her underwear on the line to dry, so the neighbors wouldn't know what kind of underwear she wore."

Dehan sighed. "So you have no idea where Pat would have run to?"

He gave a small sigh of exasperation and spread his hands. "Logically she would have gone to her brother. But that was clearly out of the question. So where *could* she go? Your detective immediately acquired access to her bank accounts and her credit cards, and as far as I know he discovered no movement on any of them."

I grunted. "But you said at the time that her clothes were missing?"

"Oh yes, well, that is to say, her favorite clothes, not all of them. She had recently bought some rather fancy pieces that were quite flattering, considering her size. She had also taken to buying more expensive makeup, and that was missing too. Her toothbrush, her toothpaste, all her toiletries were gone."

I gave my head a scratch, not because it itched, but because I was embarrassed. I had asked the question of a thousand husbands over the years, but there was something about Cyril Perkins that made the question somehow insolent, even outrageous.

"Mr. Perkins, is it possible that your wife was having an affair?"

There was real amusement in his smile and in his eyes.

"I would say that was highly unlikely."

"What makes it unlikely, Mr. Perkins?"

"I don't want to be indelicate, but she was not the most attractive woman in the world. I suppose her face was pretty, when she was smiling, which was admittedly not often. But she weighed two hundred and sixty pounds, and her personality wasn't exactly charming."

Dehan was frowning. "You married her . . ."

"Oh, yes, I did. Um . . . How can I put this? I am not exactly Hugh Jackman, or for that matter George Clooney. My first wife, I will admit freely, was a mail-order Philippine woman who actually left me and returned to the Philippines. Pat met me shortly after that, demanded sex, got pregnant, and obliged me to marry her."

"Obliged you how?"

"By appealing to my sense of morals and ethics, of course. And my reputation in the neighborhood. I am a good Catholic, Detective."

Dehan gave her head a series of little shakes, like she was clearing it. "You married her because of your reputation in the neighborhood, and because you are a Catholic?"

"Those were both factors, but not the only factors. There was also the fact that I had got her pregnant. I had a duty to care for that child." He took a deep breath and sighed. "And there was also the fact that I did not sincerely believe I would ever find anybody else. She clearly wanted to make a family with me . . ."

The shrug and the silence that followed were eloquent.

I put my hands on my knees and glanced at Dehan. Her eyebrows said she'd run out of questions, so I stood. I was about to tell him we'd let him get on when a photograph caught my eye on the mantelshelf. It was the street outside, with the Joneses' house in the background. There was a light scattering of snow, and a very pretty girl with blond hair, wrapped in a big fur coat, was standing, smiling, next to a big guy who was grinning from ear to considerable ear. He had one arm around her and was squeezing too tight. On the other side of the blonde was another girl holding on to her arm. She was also pretty, but not as glamorous.

I picked up the photograph and showed it to him. "Lilith and Ern?" He nodded. "Lilith is the blonde. The other girl is our daughter, Theresa."

"Mind if we take a picture?"

"Of course, be my guest."

Dehan took a photograph and set it back on the fireplace. We shook hands with Cyril Perkins and made our way out of his house and down the stairs to the bracing, icy cold of the street.

FOUR

WE DROVE THE SIX HUNDRED YARDS TO MARAVILLAS Bar and Grill, where we parked and hunched our way into the warm, noisy interior. There we sat beside the window, with cold ankles, eating hot potato soup and churrasco while listening to the coffee machine scream and watching the snow turn to dark sludge under the crawling traffic outside.

Dehan dunked a hunk of bread up and down a few times in her soup, until the wet bit looked like it was about to drop off, then she leaned forward and stuffed it in her mouth. She looked at me while she chewed and wiped her fingers on a paper napkin.

"It's a dead end." She said it like it was my fault, and I should feel bad about it. I frowned and tried to warm my ankles by wrapping them around each other. "What makes you say that?"

She shrugged, first with her eyebrows and then with her shoulders. "Every avenue has been explored to try to find her, Stone. It is not impossible to disappear completely in this country. Creating a new identity is comparatively easy. And her financials, you've seen the file, they just stop dead. Not a single payment from credit or debit card. Not a single withdrawal of cash."

"Her car disappeared without a trace. I don't know about

you, but I can't think of a single way to track her down. BOLOs have been issued on three separate occasions, and the FBI were notified too . . ." She shrugged and dunked her bread again. "What's left?"

I stared out at the sludge under the drooping, gray sky. After a moment I took a deep breath and shook my head. "Nope."

"Nope?"

I smiled at her and shook my head again. "Nope. Nobody disappears without a trace. The trace is there, even if we can't see it. The picture I have built up of Pat Perkins is not one of a super spy. I don't see her as a woman versed in fieldcraft, or the ways of the ninja. I don't see how she could have acquired the skills that would allow her to vanish without a trace in the way you have described, Dehan."

She stopped chewing and stared at me for a long moment.

"But she has, Stone. Maybe she found herself a boyfriend with those skills. Maybe she read a lot of John le Carré. I don't know. But the fact is she did disappear. Like that. In the way I described it."

"I didn't get a femme fatale vibe from her either."

She spooned the last of her soup out of the bowl noisily and then wiped it clean with hunks of bread, which she stuffed in her mouth. She sat back chewing and watching me. "Tho?" she said with her mouth full. "Why can'ch we find her?"

I nodded for a while, studying the half inch of beer in the bottom of my glass. "An open question," I said at last. "What is it about her disappearance that makes her so hard to find?"

She nodded and sat running her tongue over her teeth. "Yeah, that is a better question, but we still can't answer it. The fact is that however we ask it, she has disappeared without a trace, and we have no strategy available to us to find her."

"Ahhh, Ritoo Glasshopper, we don't need to find her. All we need to do is answer the question, what makes her trail so hard to find? And then, we can set about finding the trail."

"Oh." She looked at me with a perfectly expressionless face and her arms crossed over her chest. "And there was me thinking it would be difficult."

I ignored her and continued. "It seems to me that the obvious thing to do now . . ."

"Obvious . . ."

"Is to go and see Ern. Nobody was closer to her than Ern, and if anybody has any idea of where she is, it's Ern."

She raised an eyebrow at me. "Remind me how Cyril Perkins described him."

"He was very unkind. He described him as mentally retarded and subnormal. Both of which terms are frowned upon by 'Right-Thinking People.'" I put my hands on my knees and made to stand. "'Right-Thinking People' is a term upon which I myself frown, Dehan. Are you ready to brave the cold?"

"Yeah, I really didn't want a hot cup of coffee and a home-made pudding. I'd rather drive out to the St. George's Clinic for the Vulnerable and At Risk."

I smiled and stood, and she followed me out, through the flimsy red door, through the blast of cold air, and onto the icy sidewalk. We walked unsteadily to my 1964 burgundy Jaguar Mark II and climbed in.

The private clinic was in Ardsley-on-Hudson, a mile north of Dobbs Ferry. It would have been a half-hour drive, along the Bronx River Parkway and then the Mill River Parkway, but with the icy, sleeting conditions it was forty-five minutes before we turned west onto Ashford Avenue and started winding among the wintry streets of Christmas suburbia, where Santas dangled from eaves and front yards were peppered with reindeer with glowing noses, frozen in mid-step.

A few twists and turns took us to Ardsley Avenue East, where we turned right onto Broadway. The road was flanked by the parkland that surrounded the clinic, and tall, naked trees stood black and crooked against the heavy, cold sky.

Dehan had called ahead, but when we got to the tall iron gates, they were locked, and I had to climb out and press the button on the antiquated intercom. A voice asked who I was, and I told them. A moment later, the gate clicked and started to swing slowly back.

Then it was a long, asphalt drive winding through rolling lawns and copses, whitened with recent snow, to what looked like a genuine Georgian mansion. The blacktop gave way to gravel in a sweeping drive, which curved around what appeared to be an authentic Renaissance fountain but wasn't. I parked at the foot of seven broad steps that rose to an Arcadian porch, sat blinking at Dehan for a moment, and then climbed out.

Above me, seven steps away, a surprisingly flimsy door was open, and in it stood a man of about fifty, with dense hair swept back from a handsome face and his white coat open over a tweed waistcoat and pants. He raised a hand in salute, and we began to climb. As we approached, he smiled down on us and said, "Dr. James Fraser, I am the director of this clinic. Please come in out of the cold . . ."

We showed him our badges as we stepped through the door. He glanced at them without interest and ushered us through to a wood-paneled entrance hall with a reception desk on the left and a sweeping stone staircase in back.

"I'm Detective John Stone, NYPD, and this is my partner, Carmen Dehan. We phoned . . ."

"I know, please, come through to my office." He walked, pointing with an outstretched arm toward a door in the wall on the right, opposite the reception. "I confess I am intrigued as to why the NYPD might have any interest in Ernest Hartwell. The poor fellow is as inoffensive as he is huge." He laughed loudly at his own comparison, opened the door by leaning on the handle, and gave Dehan a hungry look as he said, "Please, after you."

The office was what you'd expect. It was the size of a small apartment, with triple-glazed windows and French doors leading out onto a pleasant lawn fringed by trees. The floors were dark, highly polished boards, strewn with what looked like real Persian rugs, and probably were.

His desk, which was the size of a small office and made of ancient, hand-carved oak, stood beside an open fire, in front of the French doors. He ignored it and made his way instead to a nest of Chesterfields that sat in the warm glow of the flames. He gestured to the two chairs and settled himself on the sofa. As we sat, he said, "I don't plan to be a pain in the ass about doctor-client confidentiality. Though, obviously, if disclosing any information appears to me to prejudice Ernest in any way, then I will require a court order from you. Fair enough?"

The last question was directed at Dehan and accompanied by a handsome arch of a handsome eyebrow.

I answered for her. "That's fair enough, Dr. Fraser. We're grateful for any help you can give us." I hesitated a moment, and Dehan stepped in.

"Ernest's brother-in-law, Cyril Perkins, described Ernest as subnormal and mentally retarded. Would you say that was a correct diagnosis?"

He frowned hard and pulled back, placing the palms of his hands on his knees and moving his mouth like an indignant goldfish. He made a few noises of the "wah, bah" variety and finally said, "We prefer not to view things in those terms these days. Subnormal is, if you'll forgive me, a particularly offensive term, and mentally retarded, well, I mean . . ." He laughed without amusement. "What standards are we comparing against?"

"So you wouldn't agree."

"Those are very antiquated terms, and they have no place in modern psychology and psychiatry."

She leaned forward with her elbows on her knees. "What *is* wrong with him, then?"

Mild goldfish outrage was replaced on his face by condescension and patronage. "Detective Dehan, there is *nothing* wrong with Ernest. He is a perfectly normal man who is vulnerable because his intellectual skills do not allow him to perform the social tasks that you and I take for granted. He is not *defective*, he is vulnerable. Just as a child of four is not defective, but simply in need of care and attention."

I gave a small cough and cleared my throat. "If there is nothing wrong with him, Dr. Fraser, why is he in a clinic?"

A smile that had something of the Cheshire cat about it spread across his lips. "This *is* a clinic, Detective Stone, you are quite correct, but it is also, if you read the name with care, a *refuge*. A refuge for the vulnerable and the alienated."

"Ah." I nodded. "So he is here not as a patient so much as a refugee."

"You could put it that way, indeed."

I nodded a little more. "So is he here of his own free will?"

He hesitated for a moment, then offered me a smile that said he'd decided he didn't like me. "That is, if you will forgive me, a meaningless question. Ernest has been certified as being incapable of making major life choices and decisions for himself. I compared him, if you recall, to a four-year-old child. Well, clearly, a young child cannot be asked to choose whether he wants to go to school or stay at home, buy a house or an apartment, get drunk or buy cocaine. These are choices he is not intellectually equipped to make. Equally, he is not equipped to decide whether to live alone in a small apartment in Hunts Point, or in a Georgian manor where all his needs are taken care of."

Dehan narrowed her eyes and smiled. "Not *perfectly* normal, then."

He spread his hands. "I fail to see what point you are trying to make. Ernest is here for his own protection, he is happy and well cared for. Society has a duty to protect its more vulnerable members. Hasn't it?"

"No question about that, Doc. I'm just wondering who paid for him to be certified, and who is paying for him to stay here."

He gazed at the wall and shook his head. "That, I am afraid, is one of those questions you *will* need a court order for."

I grunted. "If it becomes necessary, we might just do that. At the moment we are not actually interested in Ernest himself, but what Ernest might know without actually knowing that he knows it."

"You'll have to clarify that for me, Detective."

"Ernest's sister, Patricia, disappeared without a trace a year ago, in odd circumstances. We think Ernest might know where she is, but he might not *know* that he knows."

"You mean he might have the information that would allow you to put the pieces together and extrapolate . . ."

Dehan cut in, "Something like that. Are you aware of his having had any contact with his sister in the last year?"

He shrugged. "Not that I am aware of, Detectives, but Ernest is not a prisoner here. He has a mobile phone, and he has no restrictions on using it. We don't monitor his calls or anything of the sort. All we do is provide him with a secure environment in which he is cared for. He may well have received calls from his sister, I wouldn't know."

I thought about that for a moment, then said, "We'd like to talk to him, Dr. Fraser, have you any objection?"

He frowned for a moment, drumming his fingertips on his knees. "Not in principle, Detectives, but it depends rather on how you are going to question him. As I said, he is vulnerable, and it is my responsibility to see to his safety and well-being."

Dehan shook her head. "We just want to have a friendly chat. We're not planning on giving him the third degree or water-boarding him, Doc. Just chat for a bit and see if he knows anything that we can follow up on."

"If that's the case, then I have no objection. I'll have a nurse take you to him. The nurse will stay during your visit, and if he sees Ernest becoming distressed, he will cut the visit short. Is that understood?"

We told him it was, and he called a nurse to lead us to Ernest. The nurse was six foot six with a jaw like a kiln. He looked like he could cut most things short without trying too hard and might enjoy doing it into the bargain. He led the way without speaking and without wasting energy on facial expressions.

We found Ern in a large lounge that might once have been a ballroom. It was round, it had a high, domed ceiling and a checkerboard floor, and the outside wall was composed of tall, narrow French doors that opened out onto a sandstone terrace which overlooked formal gardens and lawns.

But instead of glittering couples swirling to the sound of Strauss waltzes, the floor was taken up with melamine and Formica tables and chairs, and a lot of unhappy-looking people in gray cardigans. They all seemed to be either knitting, watching TV, or playing checkers. Ern was knitting.

The nurse's face creased into a big smile when he saw him. "How's it going, Ern?"

Ern had a mouth like wet washing on a washing line. He offered it to his nurse in a damp smile and said, "I done another foot."

"That's cool, man. I never met nobody who knit so much as you do, Ern, or so fast. Listen, you got some visitors. They wanna chat with you fo' a while. You cool with that?"

Ern's eyes were as damp as his mouth. He looked at us each in turn and said, "Okay . . . What you want to talk about? Do you know Lilith? I had a turtle once, but it was small and it got lost."

Dehan turned to his nurse, who lost his grin and observed her through hooded eyes. She asked him, "You want to sit in and ask a few questions, or maybe just hang out nearby, where he can call you if we pull out the desk lamp?"

He didn't answer. He turned to Ern instead. "I'll be right here if you need me. Okay, Ern?"

We sat at Ern's melamine table with him while his nurse wandered over to the French doors and stood looking out at the frosted lawns. Dehan pointed at the long, amorphous coil of gray wool that trailed from Ern's needles down to the floor, by his feet.

"You did that by yourself?"

"Uh-huh, it took me all of a year, almost."

"It looks like a real cozy scarf."

"It's not a scarf. It's a cardigan."

She nodded at it for a moment, turning her frown into a smile. "Sure, I see that now that you told me. You making it for anyone special?"

"Yuh. I'm making it for me. I'm special."

"I bet you are. Is there anyone else special you can think of?"

He shrugged and looked down at his knitting, resting in his lap. "Like who?"

I said, "Like your sister, or your brother-in-law."

He raised his eyes, and they had creased up into a big smile. "Pat's special. I haven't seen her in a while, but she was real smart. She was smarter than me and Mom and Dad all put together. She was smarter than all of us put *together*," he repeated with emphasis. "Cyril is special too. He comes to see me sometimes. He takes care of me now that Pat's gone."

"You must miss Pat, right?"

"Kinda, I don't miss when she hit me!" He rocked back in his chair, laughing a big, squeaky laugh. "I don't miss when she hit me!" He said it again a couple of times, inviting us to laugh with him.

Dehan asked, "Did she hit you often?"

"Sometimes, when I made her real mad. I can be a handful sometimes. I'll tell you *that* for nothing! I can be a handful." The laughter faded, and he became serious. "She didn't like hitting people, but sometimes they made her so mad she just had to."

I asked him, "What kinds of things would you do that would make her mad, Ern?"

"Um . . ." He made an elaborate show of putting his finger on his chin and looking up at the ceiling in thought. "Things like not doing what I am told, things like being noisy, or making *disgusting* noises when I eat soup or drink my hot chocolate . . ."

"And those were the things that made Pat mad enough to hit you?"

He nodded and made a strange grunting noise for a laugh.

"You bet! She can hit real hard, and if I fell down she would kick me too. She would always say sorry after, but she explained it was my fault for not learning. Really, I should learn not to do those things. But it's hard for me to learn 'cause I inherited my mom and dad's brains. Not everyone is born smart."

"Did Cyril bring you here, to this place?"

He nodded his head. "Uh-huh. That was Cyril. He said I would be safer here, and nobody would hit me or hurt me here anymore."

Dehan leaned forward with her elbows on the table. "Ern, I want you to think very carefully before answering. Since Cyril brought you here, has Pat come to visit, or telephoned you, or been in touch with you in any way?"

He didn't need to think. He'd started shaking his head before she'd finished the question. "No, she's gone far away, as far as California."

I frowned. "California? How do you know that, Ern?"

"Cyril told me. She was always talking about moving to California. She used to get mad and say we was both as useless and stupid as each other and one day she was going to up and go to California and be free of us for good. She'd been planning that for a long time."

We were quiet for a moment, then Dehan asked him the big question. "Did she have family or friends, or anyone special in California?"

"I think so. She always used to say she had a beautiful young beach boy waiting for her there. She said she met him on holiday. She used to go there sometimes, and he was just waiting for her to go back."

I shook my head. "Have you ever told this to a cop, Ern? Have they never asked you about that?"

"No. Why would I talk to a cop? I never spoke to any cops."

"They never spoke to you?"

"No. Never."

I sighed and sank back in my chair, wondering why Cyril had

omitted this piece of information, and making a mental note to beat Mo over the head with a large stick next time I saw him. "Ern, did Pat ever mention a name? Did she ever say where this special beach boy lived?"

"Yes. She used to go on holiday to Oceanside. That's Southern California. And she met Bobby Hansen. That's what she always said: Bobby, Bobby Hansen."

FIVE

THE SUN WAS SINKING, AND THROUGH A RENT IN THE clouds burnished copper light was flooding the window and laying warped oblongs across our desk and over Dehan's face. She had her hair tied in a tight bun at the back of her neck, and I watched her, in the copper light, wondering how she could be so unaware of her own beauty.

She was looking through Pat Perkins' financials for the last two years and spoke without looking up.

"You done?"

I blinked, like I was coming out of a trance. "Huh?"

"Staring at me."

"Was I? I was thinking about something else," I lied.

She smiled at Pat Perkins' financials because she knew I was lying.

"Yeah? What were you thinking about?" Then, without pausing, "This woman has not spent a dime in the last twelve months. At least not from her credit card or her current account."

I looked around the room. There was a sad tree in one corner draped with limp tinsel. I regarded it a moment and asked, "Do you know how many Robert Hansens there are in California?"

She sighed deeply and slowly, shaking her head. "Couple of thousand?"

"Two hundred and ninety-eight. At an average of two minutes per phone call, that is five hundred and ninety-six minutes, divided by sixty makes it just short of ten hours, and all but two minutes of that time will be unproductive. Like Edison proving how not to make a light bulb."

She twitched an eyebrow. "That's police work, boss."

I picked up the internal phone and called the inspector. When he answered, it was with an agreeable sigh, like I was the nicest thing that had happened to him all day.

"John, how are you?"

"Well, sir, a little overworked."

"Do you need time off?"

"No, sir, just a couple of rookies to make some phone calls for me. It's the Pat Perkins case."

"Ah, yes, tricky. Woman vanished without a trace."

"Yeah, well, we've been talking to her brother, and he recalls she used to talk about one Bobby Hansen in California. Trouble is, phoning every Robert Hansen in Cali is going to have me on the phone for days, and I have another avenue I would like to explore . . ."

"Of course, John. Why not rope in Chavez and Vazquez? Get them calling, brief them on what to say, and you explore those other avenues you're interested in. If you have a hunch, John, I am certain it's a good one."

"Thank you, sir."

I hung up and called Maria, the desk sergeant, and told her to find me Vazquez and Chavez, then confronted Dehan's hostile stare across the desk.

"What 'other avenues'?"

I told her what I was thinking. She gazed out at the failing light, which had started to tinge the burnished bronze with pink, and said quietly, "His ex-wife? That is some leap, Stone. You're out of your mind."

"You think so? Isn't that a thing ex-wives and girlfriends do? Don't they get in contact with each other to compare horror stories? Can't you see Pat doing that?"

She shook her head. "She's in the Philippines."

"An email away. A phone call away."

"I think it's too soon to be clutching at straws, Stone. I think California is more likely to be a fruitful search, despite your excuses to the chief."

"Too soon, huh? Well, Dehan, just remember this, my girl. The biggest bug may be under the smallest stone."

"Really?" She dropped her file on the desk and reached for the phone. "I'm going to call the California PDs, put out a new BOLO on the car, though it probably has California plates now."

"Hmmm . . . good idea," I said and didn't move. She stopped with her hand on the receiver and stared at me. "What are you thinking? You think it's a waste of time, don't you? Why do you think it's a waste of time?"

"No, no, not at all!" I shook my head. "Police work, as you observed yourself but a few moments ago, is all about good procedure. The fact that the car will probably have had a respray and new plates, and is one of the most common cars in the States, is neither here nor there. While you do that, I am going to waste some time of my own, and then, Ritoo Glasshopper, we should go and see Pat and Cyril's daughter, Theresa."

She glowered at me, like a thunderhead. "She wasn't even there. She was working."

"But she may have an insight, Dehan, into where her mother has gone. Small stones, big bugs."

She picked up the receiver. "If you say so, Sensei, but I figure she's going to tell us exactly what she told Mo a year ago."

I shrugged and switched on my laptop. "That's cold cases, Dehan."

I worked in silence for a little more than half an hour while Dehan called the various California PDs. From what I eavesdropped, they didn't seem to be very receptive. I couldn't blame them. A Toyota RAV4 isn't exactly a rare car, and when you add to that the fact that the plates had probably been changed and the car repainted, there wasn't a hell of a lot you could Be on the Lookout for.

When she finally hung up, Dehan looked frazzled. She did a fair impression of a Californian and said, "'Well, ma'am, what exactly is it you'd like us to look out for? Toyota RAV4 with unknown plates and an unknown color? Well, we have about a hundred thousand of them.' Jerk!"

"I won't say I told you so." I offered her a smile that said I had done what I thought to be some useful research and sent what I figured would be some useful emails, and I felt quietly smug. I picked up my cell, looked at the clock, and pointed at her across the desk. "You, my dear, need a stiff martini. I shall heat up what is left of last night's moussaka."

"Sold."

I dialed, and it began to ring. "And tomorrow we go and see . . ."

The ringing stopped almost immediately, and a crisp, feminine voice spoke.

"Theresa Perkins."

"Dr. Theresa Perkins?"

"Yes, this is she. Who is this please?"

"Detective John Stone of the NYPD. We are investigating your mother's disappearance . . ."

There was a moment's silence, then, "You mean you are hunting her for the murder of Lilith Jones."

I smiled even though she couldn't see me. "That is not what I mean, and it's not what I said. I run a cold-case unit here at the Forty-Third, and we are taking a fresh look at the case. We are trying to approach it with an open mind."

"Well, that's not going to be easy. All the circumstantial evidence and the forensic evidence points to my mother. The fact that she disappeared on the night of the murder doesn't help."

"But it's not conclusive, Dr. Perkins, and until we get some kind of proof, we need to keep an open mind. What I was actually hoping was that you could spare us ten or fifteen minutes tomorrow to discuss the case with us."

"I doubt I can tell you much more than I told your detective at the time. I wasn't there."

"A cold-case investigation tends to approach things differently, Dr. Perkins. It would be a great help to have your input . . ."

She sighed noisily through her nose. "I have a private surgery opposite the Harlem Hospital, at number five thirty-one, Lenox Avenue. I'm free between nine and ten. Please be on time; at eleven I go on duty at the hospital."

I thanked her and hung up.

Dehan was watching me through narrowed eyes.

"You just called her now. What have you been doing for the last half hour?"

Outside, darkness had eased in on dusk's coattails, and a brisk breeze had kicked up. I frowned at the dark glass of the window and cupped a hand to my ear. "What is that?"

"What?"

"A voice, calling. It seems to say, *Deeeehaaaaan! Deeee-haaaan!* I do believe it is the voice of a dry martini . . ."

She didn't answer until she'd stood, pulled on her coat and woolly hat, and wrapped her scarf around her throat and face, then she said, "Jerk."

We made our way out into the icy night and walked unsteadily to the old Jaguar. We climbed in and slammed the doors, trapping in the cold. I turned the key in the ignition, and the big old cat roared to life. As I backed out of the lot, Dehan spoke through several layers of wool.

"Okay, I get that there is a chance Pat might have stayed in touch with Theresa. She's her daughter. But, here's the thing, if she knows where her mother is, she is either A, going to tell us or B, not going to tell us."

"So far there is no contradicting you."

"Shut up. If she were going to tell us, she would have done it by now, and if she is not going to tell us, there is nothing we can do, as far as I can see, that will induce her to. She is, after all, protecting her mother."

"There we part company." I crawled through the sludge to the end of Story Avenue and pulled onto Soundview. "If she does know something about her mother's whereabouts, she may well be concealing it from us because she believes her mother to be the prime suspect."

"Correctly so."

"Indeed. However, if she were to believe that our aim is to protect or exonerate her mother . . ."

"*Protect* her? *Exonerate* her?" She frowned at me through layers of woolly reindeer, and the pom-pom on her hat bounced. "Stone, we can't protect her mother, or exonerate her! We need to arrest her and prosecute her. The woman murdered a young girl! Stabbed her in the back with a pair of scissors!"

"Innocent till proven guilty, Dehan."

She pulled her scarf down to reveal her lips. "Come on, Stone, climb back down the ladder of abstraction to the world of actual facts. There are no other suspects. Lilith Jones was found outside Pat's house with Pat's scissors stuck in her back. Pat hated Lilith, was jealous of her, and Pat and her car have not been seen since. She is the only person who had motive, opportunity, and means. How on God's green Earth are you going to make Theresa believe that we are going to protect and exonerate her?"

We drove in silence for a moment, past the warm glow of the shop fronts, bright with red, green, and blue Christmas decorations, that reflected wet on the pavements and the blacktop among the slow-falling sleet.

Dehan added suddenly, "Without lying to her."

After a moment I said, "Well, okay, imagine Pat witnessed the murder and fled."

She pulled off her hat, making long strands of static hair stand up from her head, and stared at me. "You're serious . . ."

"Sure, why not?"

"Because all the evidence points . . ."

"I know where the evidence points, Dehan, but ask yourself this: Who is your prime witness?"

She took a deep breath, held it a moment, and said, "Gwen Jones."

"The victim's mother. Did she see the murder committed? Was she able to identify the killer?"

"No. You know she wasn't."

"So the evidence points, but it does not convict."

"You're being pedantic."

"Perhaps, Dehan, but when convicting a person accused of murder, it pays to be pedantic. The fact is, compelling as the very little evidence we have is, there are aspects of the case that are very unsatisfactory."

She looked at me sidelong, but her expression had changed. She thrust out her lower lip and stared out the windshield where, with a desultory thud, the wipers occasionally swept away the accumulating sleet.

"I guess," she said at last.

I gave a small shrug. "It's not just about what the evidence says, Dehan. It is often about what it fails to say."

After a moment she nodded at a passing 24/7 and muttered, "You're deep, Stone. It's one of the things I love about you."

I smiled at her, and she grinned out the window. "Stop smiling at me. I'm shy." I laughed, and she went on quickly, "What the evidence *doesn't* say, like, for example . . . ?"

"Well, for a start, disappearing so completely requires careful planning . . ."

"And there is now new evidence that she may have been planning it for some time."

"True, from Ern, no less; but the murder—the actual act itself —was purely spontaneous, unplanned, and apparently brought on by a fit of rage." She grunted, and I continued. "Also, having planned it all so well and so thoroughly, she left her scissors stuck in Lilith's back with her prints all over them. How difficult would it have been to pull out the scissors and either take them with her or wash them and replace them?"

She nodded and made a "you have a point" face. I continued.

"And there's another thing that makes me uncomfortable. Cyril was confused when he got home by the fact that she had not cleared the table. She is apparently pretty OCD, which is consistent with the meticulous planning of her disappearance. Yet, if she was preparing to clear the table, as we must assume she was, what the hell was she doing with the sewing box? Surely there must have been plenty of knives on the table, not least the one they used to carve the turkey!" I paused while she stared at me, and stopped at a red light. "Also, if she was, following her obsessive-compulsive tendencies, clearing the table . . ." I shook my head. "The dining room is in the back of the house. How did she know that Lilith was walking past at that time? What the hell was she doing at the front window with the sewing box?"

The lights changed to green, and I pulled away. Dehan said, "They are questions we are not going to be able to answer until we find Pat."

I nodded. "They are questions I want to put to Theresa tomorrow, before I ask her if she has any contact with her mother. I am also going to ask her something else."

"What?"

"I'm going to ask her to contact her mother on our behalf and tell her that we do not think she committed the murder."

"What the hell, Stone?"

"Then we'll give it a week and request her phone records, see whom she called."

"But what possible suspect can you have aside from her? Whoever killed Lilith had access to Pat's sewing basket. That narrows the field quite a bit, to . . ." She shrugged and shook her head.

I interrupted. "Robert Hansen?"

"*What?*"

"Do you know for a fact that he wasn't here at the time?"

"No, but we have no reason to believe he was, Stone!"

"Except that it doesn't make sense that Pat killed Lilith, and somebody else must have had access to her sewing basket."

"But why the hell would Robert Hansen want to kill Lilith Jones?"

"Because she saw him?"

She turned in her seat to stare at me. "What are you saying, Stone?"

"I'm just answering your questions, Dehan. I'm making it up as I go along, but, off the top of my head, it *is* a possibility. The point is, it is not impossible that there is another actor in this drama, somebody who took Pat's scissors and killed Lilith. And, seeing she was in the frame . . ."

"She and the killer fled together . . ."

"I'm just saying that's one of a number of possibilities. All the evidence we have seems to point one way. But the evidence we have doesn't answer some awkward questions. So we need to keep an open mind."

"And we need to transmit that to Theresa tomorrow morning, in the hope that she will help us if she thinks she can clear her mother."

I gave a single nod. "That is about the size of it, yes."

She wrapped her scarf around her mouth again and pulled her hat back on her head.

"You're deep," she said quietly, through layers of wool. Then, after a while, "So, if you're right, if we find Robert Hansen, we'll find Pat too."

I nodded slowly. "It's possible."

"And that suggests," she went on, "that if she had indeed been planning to dump her family for a long time, and Hansen had shown up to take her away, whatever plan they had was scuppered when Lilith saw Hansen. And the fact that Hansen killed Lilith when she saw him would suggest that the plan they had involved more than just eloping. Jesus! Lilith may have unwittingly given her life, Stone, to save Cyril's!"

I drew breath to answer, but she pointed her finger at me like a gun.

"We should narrow the search of Robert Hansens and look for Robert Hansens who have a record, especially of violent crime."

I closed my mouth and nodded. "That is a good idea. We'll keep Vazquez on all Robert Hansens, but we'll get Chavez looking at those who have a rap sheet."

She nodded. "Good. See? That's why you're older than me. Now get me home and make me that martini. Why the hell are you driving so slow?"

SIX

Next morning the clouds had broken here and there, and patches of cold blue sky shone through, making the blacktop and the sidewalks bright with melted snow and sleet. At nine a.m. we turned off East 135th onto Malcolm X Boulevard, which is also, confusingly, Lenox Avenue, and I parked outside the Harlem Temple Community Center. We crossed the road on careful feet, because the blacktop was still icy, and pushed through the street door into the warmth of a small, clean foyer.

We rode the elevator to the second floor and stepped out into a short passage that was carpeted in the kind of mildly depressing sage green that makes you sigh and wish you were somewhere else. An old-fashioned wrought iron railing skirted a spiral stairwell on the right, and on the left there was a long passage with evenly spaced doors. Most of them had brass plates outside proclaiming the owner to be some kind of medical specialist. Theresa's stood out because she wasn't a specialist in anything yet.

Her door was open, and we pushed through into an ante-room with an empty desk that had an empty chair behind it. Other chairs flanked the walls, and in the corner there was a lonely, plastic Christmas tree. A second door stood open too, and through it I could see Theresa. She had on her white coat, and a stethoscope hung around her neck. She was sitting at her surprisingly handsome desk reading through what looked like a report. On the desk there was a laptop, a mug with pens, and a couple of framed photographs. In her hand she had a cup of coffee poised halfway between a saucer and her mouth. Her attention was fixed on the papers in front of her.

I approached and stood in the doorway. Opposite her, across the desk, there were two bentwood chairs. To her left, beside the window, there was a filing cabinet with a couple of framed photographs on it. To her right, beside a sofa, standing grim against the wall, grinning maliciously at me, was a skeleton on a stand. A few posters decorated the walls proclaiming the advisability of condoms and a healthy diet.

Dehan stood beside me and knocked. Theresa looked up.

"Dr. Perkins? I'm Detective Carmen Dehan. This is my partner, Detective John Stone . . ."

Theresa sagged back in her chair and sighed. She didn't say anything but gestured to the chairs opposite her and slipped the report away into a manila folder. I followed Dehan into the room, and we sat.

"Detectives, I don't mean to be rude, but I am extremely busy. I have a free clinic this morning, and then I am on call at the hospital for the next twenty-four hours. On top of that, I have an article to write and an insurmountable mountain of paperwork to get through. I really don't know how you think I can help you."

I studied her face a moment. She looked pale and drawn.

"Dr. Perkins, I'll get straight to the point: the detectives in the initial investigation were convinced that your mother murdered Lilith and then fled. She is the prime suspect in this case."

"She's the only suspect in the case. It's the obvious inference to be drawn from the facts, Detective Stone. I hope you're not going to insult my intelligence by pretending you don't believe that."

I smiled. "You're right. It is the obvious inference to be drawn from the facts, and we have no intention of insulting your intelligence. However, there are inconsistencies in the evidence that lead me to wonder whether the original team weren't a little hasty."

She sipped her coffee, watching me. "Like what?"

It was Dehan who answered.

"Ern led us to believe that your mother might have been planning to do a bunk for some time . . ."

Only her eyes shifted. "You spoke to Uncle Ernest?"

Dehan gave a small nod. "If what he told us is true, and she had been planning to go for some time, that would certainly explain how she has managed to disappear so thoroughly without leaving a trace. That is not an easy thing to do. Would you agree with him? Did she talk a lot about leaving?"

She nodded once. "Yes. She used to say that she was going to go to California. She'd had a holiday love affair there once. She went back a few times. It was a way of getting at my dad."

"Can you remember the guy's name?"

"Of course. She used to talk about him all the time, trying to make Dad jealous. His name was Bobby Hansen. She went on about how he was a *real* man, and what a good lover he was."

She paused, gazing over at the window. After a moment she said, "Oceanside, halfway between Los Angeles and San Diego. She was always talking about how one day she would disappear and go back with Bobby. Whenever she got mad, which was most days, she'd start on about how he'd always been crazy about her, he appreciated her, he wanted her back. And when she left and went back with him, then we'd miss her and realize what we'd lost." She made a sour smile. "I promise you I don't miss her, and I sure as hell don't feel I've lost anything. She was not a nice woman, and she made our lives a misery."

Dehan asked her, "How likely is it that she was in fact in touch with this Robert Hansen?"

Theresa made a face, drew down the corners of her mouth,

and shrugged. "I always thought it was bullshit, and she only said it to torture Dad. But when she vanished like that, I thought maybe it was true." She glanced at me and added, "Some men are into fat bitches. There's no accounting for taste." Her eyes drifted back to the window. "My dad must have gone for her at some time, else I wouldn't be here now, would I?"

"Okay." Dehan rubbed her cheek and frowned. "So, let's say for argument's sake that she was in touch with Bobby Hansen. It's possible that between them they put together some kind of plan so that she could leave her family and disappear. The problem is that, if that *is* the case, Lilith's murder makes very little sense. It's chaotic, ill thought out." She paused, watching Theresa, who was watching her back. Dehan went on, "You have on the one hand this careful, meticulous plan to disappear carried out to perfection—" She gestured with her left hand, as though setting down the plan in the air. Then she repeated the gesture with her right hand. "And then you have this chaotic, random killing, which serves no practical purpose."

Theresa sat chewing her lip. She didn't say anything, and I cut in.

"It's my understanding, Dr. Perkins, that your mother suffered to some degree from obsessive-compulsive disorder."

"It was never diagnosed, but she is obsessive and compulsive about cleanliness and order. She becomes deeply anxious if things are not arranged exactly as she wants them."

"Which makes it extremely unlikely, doesn't it, that she would be standing at the front window, with her sewing box, while the dinner table was covered in the remains of the Christmas lunch. It is also very unlikely that she would leave her scissors, covered in her own fingerprints, stuck in Lilith's back."

She nodded, then gave a small shrug. "She might have panicked . . ." But there was very little conviction in her voice, or in her expression. I asked her, "Would that be consistent with her obsessive-compulsive behavior?"

She didn't react for a moment, then gave her head a small, noncommittal shake. "No, not really."

"So, you see, there are a few small things like that which we are finding it hard to reconcile. I'm not saying that Pat didn't kill Lilith, but what I am saying is that I am far from convinced that she did." I sighed. "It may be that she is hiding from a crime that somebody else committed, and she feels she is somehow in the frame. And however you feel about her as a person, that would mean that whoever killed Lilith is still at large."

Theresa didn't answer straightaway. Her face, already pale, had become drawn and pasty. She reached out and adjusted the file on her desk so that it aligned with the edge.

"You're hoping that maybe she stayed in touch with me, being her daughter, and that, if I believe you no longer have her as your prime suspect, I might lead you to her."

I nodded. "I'm not going to lie to you, Dr. Perkins. That is exactly what I am hoping."

She sat smiling at the edge of the file. Finally she said, "You hope that, because you still haven't grasped exactly who my mother is." She raised her eyes to meet Dehan's. "My mother is the most cruel, stone-hearted bitch you are ever likely to meet on this Earth. I exist in this world exclusively because she wanted a hook with which to catch my father, and I was that hook. She didn't abort me once he'd married her simply because she feared he would divorce her if she did. She never tired of telling me how much I had made her suffer, and how I had ruined her life.

"How and why my father ever loved her are two questions that I shall never be able to answer. They are beyond my understanding. She must have satisfied some guilt-ridden, masochistic weakness in his deep psyche, but don't let his feelings for her fool you. That woman was a monster, and she had as little maternal feeling for me, and as little love for Dad, as she had for those scissors she used to kill Lilith."

Dehan shook her head, narrowing her eyes. "But if that is

true, her motive for killing Lilith becomes a nonsense. If she didn't kill her out of jealousy, why did she kill her?"

Theresa laughed, and for a moment I saw her father's humorous intelligence in her face. "*Does* it become a nonsense?" she said. "I don't think so at all. I think it is exactly the opposite. It makes perfect sense. A good person, a person with humanity and decency, even when driven mad with jealousy, will stop well short of the urge to actually kill another human being. They may think about it, but they will not yield to that impulse.

"But a heartless monster, a narcissistic egomaniac like my mother, doesn't *need* jealousy in order to be driven to an act of murder!" She raised both hands palm out and closed her eyes. "That is, let me explain. Jealousy, as we understand it, involves three people: ourselves, the person we love, and a person who threatens to take our loved one away. But in the case of my mother, jealousy involves only *two* people: herself and somebody who might outshine her."

Dehan said, "Lilith."

Theresa nodded. "Lilith was a sweet, beautiful, kindhearted person. I had grown up with her. She was like a sister to me. Dad was really fond of her. Everybody was. She was in *every respect* the opposite of my mother. She was kind, affectionate, loving, compassionate, and *beautiful*! And that was enough for Mom to start breeding that disgusting, black loathing in her heart—or whatever it is she has instead of a heart. She had watched Lilith grow over the years from a sweet kid into a beautiful young woman. *That* alone was enough for her to want to kill her."

I gave my head a single small shake. "That is a very damning assessment. Are you sure of what you are saying?"

She didn't bother answering. Instead she said, "I wasn't there that day, I tended to avoid spending Christmas with her whenever possible, but Dad told me afterwards everything that happened. I was shocked by Lilith's death, obviously, but when I discovered everything that had happened, I can't say I was exactly surprised.

Shocked, but not surprised. It was a brutal, ugly act that was in perfect keeping with her personality."

"Where do you think she is, Dr. Perkins?"

She shrugged again and glanced at her watch. "I always assumed she was in California, but I actually have no idea." She hesitated a moment. "The fact is I received a few postcards from her, three in total, about a month after she disappeared. They were postmarked Los Angeles. I should have handed them over to the police, but I was so angry with her, and so happy to be free of her, that I screwed them up and threw them in the trash. I didn't even read them. After that I heard no more from her."

I sighed. "So there is no point in my telling you that, if you are in touch with her, I'd like you to give her a message, that we are far from convinced of her guilt and we want to help her."

She gave a small, surprisingly pretty laugh. "Well, Detective Stone, you have just done that very thing, haven't you? But you're right, there was no point. I am not in touch with her, and if I were, I would have informed the police long ago. I was not fond of my mother, but I was very fond of Lilith."

I scratched my chin. There was something nagging at the back of my mind, and I couldn't quite square it.

"Who else was important in Lilith's life, Dr. Perkins? The way you describe her: beautiful, charming, loving . . . There must have been plenty of men interested in her. Did she have a boyfriend?"

She offered Dehan a lopsided smile. "This is the wonderful arrogance of men. If a man is handsome, he must be a 'dawg' and a heartbreaker. If a woman is beautiful and charming, she must have a boyfriend or a husband. Did it occur to you, Detective Stone, that maybe Lilith was not attracted to the men who were attracted to her?"

Dehan snorted, and I smiled pleasantly at Theresa. "Leaving my primeval attitudes on one side, Dr. Perkins, the question is, did Lilith have a boyfriend?"

"Yes. I never met him, and I have no idea who he was. I do

recall that she sometimes spoke of a boyfriend, though. I should have thought you'd be better off asking her mother about that."

Dehan answered. "We did. She didn't know anything about him either. Apparently Lilith didn't want him to meet her mother because her mother was weird."

She gave her pretty laugh again. "Well, that doesn't surprise me much. Gwen is a nice woman as far as it goes, but she used to give Lilith a pretty hard time. She accused her, often, of being shallow and narcissistic, which would seem to be a more accurate description of Gwen than it ever was of Lilith. So it isn't really surprising that Lilith didn't share intimate things with her mother."

I nodded a few times and made to stand.

"Thank you, Dr. Perkins, you have actually been very helpful."

I got to my feet, and Dehan followed suit. Theresa stood too and spread her hands.

"I'm sorry I wasn't able to tell you what you wanted to hear, but the fact is, Mom and I were never close. I don't think anybody was ever very close with Mom."

She said it as she watched me step over to the filing cabinet and pick up one of the photographs that stood there. It showed Cyril and Theresa standing beside a gray Toyota RAV4. Theresa was dressed in a graduation cap and gown and was holding her degree, bound with a blue ribbon.

Next to it was a picture of Theresa in a backyard somewhere, sitting on a deck chair in the shade of a tree. She was holding a small baby, and crouched beside her, oblivious to the camera, was a man of about forty, kissing the baby's head.

She spoke abruptly. "My husband and my baby, shortly after Mom left. I am trying not to make the same mistakes my mother made. Or my father."

I pointed to the gray Toyota. "That her car? The one she took with her?"

"Yes."

Dehan was studying the photographs. She spoke without taking her eyes from them. I was surprised when she said, "You should have handed those postcards over to the cops." Now she turned and held her eye. "We might have traced her with them."

Theresa shrugged. She didn't look especially contrite.

"I didn't think. I was just happy to have her out of my life, and I didn't want her getting in touch or coming back."

"Did you want to catch Lilith's killer?"

She didn't answer, and shortly after that we left.

SEVEN

WE STEPPED OUT INTO THE ICY MORNING SUNSHINE. The sun was low in the south, gleaming against the glass and steel of the hospital. Dehan took my arm, and we turned left along the boulevard, crunching over half-melted sludge toward Miss Melanie's Spoonbread Too.

"What if . . ." she said.

I waited and after a while glanced down at her. She was staring down at her feet as she picked her way over the gray, stained ice. I smiled. "That has the makings of a good question."

"What if Theresa wasn't working that Christmas?"

"Easy enough to find out, but I'm not sure where you're going with that."

She didn't answer but kept watching her boots for a while until we reached the door of the café. She pushed in, and I grabbed a table by the window, under a strand of tinsel and a blue ball, while she ordered two coffees and some blueberry pie. As she set them down on the table and sat, she said:

"Lilith went out after the Christmas meal to take some food to Mrs. Rodriguez, on the corner of Gildersleeve, remember? Mrs. Rodriguez is dead now, so we can't check, but Gwen says Lilith was gone from about four till seven thirty or eight."

I was curious and frowned to show it. "Yes . . ."

"But it was seven thirty when Gwen actually called Mrs. Rodriguez. So that is three and a half hours. Cyril never actually specified at what time he took Ern home. He just said after lunch, and he never told us at what time he got back."

"That's true."

"And according to Gwen, when she called Mrs. Rodriguez, all she said was that Lilith had left at least half an hour earlier."

"What's your point, Dehan?"

She stared at me a moment, then took a big spoonful of blueberry pie and stuffed it in her mouth. She sat staring at me and chewing. I gave a small sigh and sipped my coffee. She said:

"Be ashly hub no weal chime fwame fo je mwada."

"We have no real time frame for the . . ."

She swallowed and spoke at the same time.

"Murder."

"Between four and seven thirty."

"Probably. But it could just as easily be three and eight or eight thirty."

"Okay. Dehan, you're driving at something. What is it?"

"What if Lilith met with her boyfriend that evening?" My frown deepened. She went on, with more pie in her mouth. "Ashtwa sheeing msh Wodwigesh . . ."

I rolled my eyes. "After seeing Mrs. Rodriguez, she took the food 'round, then snuck out, either with or without Mrs. Rodriguez's complicity, and had a rendezvous with her man." Dehan nodded. I went on. "I have just one question: What would she do that for, what possible reason have you for thinking she did, and where does it get us?"

She narrowed her eyes and raised three fingers at me. I sighed and cut my pie with my fork.

"Okay, Gwen could be very controlling and perhaps gave Lilith a hard time about not spending Christmas with her. Also, as she told us, she didn't want her man to meet her weird mother.

So Mrs. Rodriguez would be a useful excuse to get away and see her lover boy."

"But what reason have you for thinking she might have done that? I mean, what objective evidence?"

She sipped her coffee, and I fed myself pie. We sat staring at each other. She didn't say anything, so I shrugged.

"Granted, three hours or more is a long time for a lively young girl to be sitting with a rather elderly lady at Christmas. An hour would probably have been most people's limit, especially on a full stomach. She had a boyfriend, and they were probably pretty keen to see each other. If he was local, they might well have used that opportunity . . . Okay, Dehan, I see your point, and it is at least worth exploring the possibility . . ."

I sipped coffee, picked up what was left of the pie slice, and bit into it.

"But even if it is true, and it is pure speculation at this point, where does it get us? Let's not forget that they were Pat's scissors in Lilith's back, covered in Pat's prints . . ."

I trailed off, and Dehan nodded. "He would have had to have access to Pat's house and her sewing box."

I shook my head. "No. It's too far-fetched . . ."

"But there is something there, Stone. I can't see it, but I can feel it. There was somebody else there . . ."

I shook my head again with more conviction. "But what are we saying, Dehan? That Lilith's boyfriend, for some unfathomable reason, broke into Pat's house, stole her scissors, stabbed Lilith in the back, and then abducted Pat, leaving absolutely no trace?"

She stared out the window, chewing her bottom lip. "No . . . But it is a long time, Stone. What was she doing all that time?"

I sighed, shrugged, and shook my head. "Maybe they were watching TV."

"For three hours?"

"I don't know. What was on that night? You said yourself the time frame was unclear. Maybe it was only two hours."

She shook her head and pointed at me. "The scissors don't square up, Stone. You said so yourself. Neither does the amount of time she was away. Something else happened that night, and it was not Lilith strolling past on her way home, Pat catching a glimpse of her through the window and rushing out to stab her in the back. Something else happened, and that something else was the *same* something that kept Lilith away from home for three hours."

I sighed and picked up my coffee. "You're preaching to the choir, Dehan. It was me who pointed out the weakness in Mo's theory to begin with, remember? But inferring that Lilith met her boyfriend and he killed her with Pat's scissors, from the fact that we don't know exactly how long she was out, is pushing it a bit."

"Okay . . ." She nodded for a bit. "Fine, but I am not *inferring* that. I'm saying, what if? What if she met someone? It places an unknown actor at the scene, which is something we both sensed from the beginning. Am I wrong?"

"No."

"Let's go visit her job. See if we can get a handle on her boyfriend. We find him, and at the very least, Stone, I guarantee we will have a better idea of what happened that night. The Christian Faith Thrift Shop, 1213 Pugsley Avenue, if memory serves."

I stared out the window, at all the legs and shoes trudging over the mulch of water, carbon, and general filth in the air. "And she was training to be a nurse." I turned and looked at Dehan. "Do you remember where?"

She shook her head. "No."

"What do you want to bet . . . ?"

We sat staring at each other for a while. It was a habit we had fallen into over time. It made other people uncomfortable, but it helped us think. After a moment she looked away and muttered, "Shit . . ." Then she looked back at me. "What does it mean? It doesn't make sense."

I sighed and got to my feet. "Maybe. Let's go talk to her workmates and check the file. Murder never makes sense, Dehan, except to the killer."

We took the Madison Avenue Bridge and headed east along the expressway. Neither of us spoke. My head was full suddenly of what had become so obvious it could not be ignored, but at the same time, as Dehan had said, what was obvious made no sense at all.

At Soundview I came off onto Bruckner Boulevard and turned onto White Plains Road. Right, onto Watson, brought me to Pugsley, and four blocks north brought me to the Christian Faith Thrift Shop. I pulled up outside, into a drift of ice and sludge, and we climbed out. Dehan crossed the sidewalk without waiting for me, but she paused, holding the door open till I caught up with her. Then she stepped through the gloom and jumble of the shop, up to the counter where a middle-aged woman in a neat bun and a blue cardigan stood watching us over the top of her reading glasses. Dehan already had her badge in her hand.

"Detective Dehan, NYPD. This is Detective Stone. Do you run this shop?"

The woman managed to convey that Dehan was a very badly brought up little girl without altering her facial expression even a little. She seemed merely to cool her eyes down to slightly below freezing.

"I am," she said. "I am Mrs. Peabody, the manager."

"Mrs. Peabody, how long have you worked here?"

"I have worked here for fifteen years. Now would you *kindly* tell me what this is about?"

"It's about Lilith Jones. Do you remember her?"

Her face softened somewhat. "Of course I remember Lilith. She was a very sweet, capable child. It was an absolute tragedy, what happened to her. How can I help you?"

I said, "We are interested in making contact with her close friends, in particular any boyfriend she might have had. Are you aware of her having had a boyfriend?"

There were several bodies in large coats moving slowly through the shop, inspecting old coffeepots, paperbacks, boxes of dead Christmas decorations, and clothes. Behind Mrs. Peabody there was an arch, and as she drew breath to reply, a skinny boy in black jeans leaned out. He was fitting a black velvet evening dress onto a hanger and had hair like a meringue piled on top of his head. He stared at her as she answered me.

"Well, of course, she *was* popular. She was charming, bright, funny, and of course extremely beautiful."

The boy in the arch with the black velvet evening dress sighed and rolled his eyes. "*Ravishing*," he said. "Those *eyes*! To *die* for!"

Apart from a small wince, Mrs. Peabody continued as though he had not spoken. "Certainly we were all friends, though I am not sure any of us was an actual, what do they call them these days? BFF?" She turned to the meringue. "Nigel? Were you aware of any special friends of Lilith's? Any boyfriends?"

He came and leaned his hip against the counter. "Friends, any number. Everybody adored her. *Intimate* friends, not a one. She was so *hard* to get close to, and believe me, I tried. As to a boyfriend, she did talk about a boyfriend, some lucky boy she was going to marry, but she never brought him here or introduced him. She was awfully private." He gave Mrs. Peabody a burning glance and raised an eyebrow. "You might even say *secretive*, Maude, don't you think?"

Maude Peabody sighed. "I think you are dramatizing a little, Nigel. She was certainly a private person and was happier to listen than to talk." From behind her Nigel grimaced and shook his head. She went on. "I don't think she kept her boyfriend secret so much as private. I did hear her mention him once or twice. She seemed to be very much in love, but to be honest I didn't pay much attention, and I never got the impression it was a serious affair. Perhaps a little one-sided. More to do with what she dreamed of, than what was actually *happening*."

Nigel rolled his eyes and went to hang the dress on a rack.

Dehan said, "So he never turned up to collect her from work or anything like that."

Nigel answered by calling across the shop, "*Heavens* no! Besides, the only place she ever went from here was to her *real* job at the hospital."

Maude Peabody cut in. "You know how it is with doctors and nurses. They work all the hours that God sends, and the poor souls have no time for a social life, or for that matter to develop a real relationship."

I nodded like I had a lot of experience with doctors and nurses and their underdeveloped relationships. "So did you get the impression her boyfriend might be someone at the hospital?"

Maude made a face that said she was doubtful, but it was an interesting idea. Nigel spoke forcefully to the dress rack. He said, "Yup! That is *precisely* the idea I got."

Dehan pulled her cell from her pocket and thumbed through the photographs. While she did it, she asked, "Did anybody at all ever show up for her? Either to deliver her, collect her, or just drop in and say hello?"

Maude sighed. "It's possible, but it was over a year ago now . . ."

"It's *exactly* a year, Maude." Nigel hurried over. "Oooh, photos! What are we looking at?"

She showed them the picture of Lilith and Ern outside the Joneses' house. "You never saw this guy here?"

"Good Lord, no! What *is* he?"

Maude scowled at him. "*Nigel!* My goodness!"

"Well forgive me for *breathing*! And having eyes in my head! Never saw *him*, but that one"—he pointed elaborately at Theresa —"she came in a few times. She drives an original, red Mini Cooper, at *least* forty years old, and she picked Lilith up regularly, for sure."

Dehan glanced at me. I said, "They ever say where they were going? To meet friends or something?"

Maude shook her head, and Nigel sighed and rolled his eyes

again. "My *God,* Maude! I can't *believe* you! They didn't go out, though it *was* mostly Fridays. They worked together. Lilith was training as a nurse at the Harlem, and this one"—he tapped Theresa in the photo—"was a doctor there. I imagine they were carpooling."

"Nigel, you're such a gossip!"

"That may be so, darling, but I am sure the detectives have found *me* more useful than your most proper, reserved, and demure self!" He turned back to us. "But if anybody can tell you who her boyfriend was, it will be that girl there. They were tight. Believe me, I *know* people!"

"The fact is, Detectives"—Maude waved a hand to silence him —"aside from that young lady, whom I gathered was a childhood friend, nobody ever came to pick her up, much less see her at the shop." She smiled without humor. "And that may have something to do with the fact that we are so busy here."

"Yeah, I get that." Dehan looked around at the scattered customers who still seemed to be gazing at the same items. "We get pretty busy too, investigating homicides, you know."

The frozen smile didn't shift. "If we could help . . ."

"Yeah, you have a merry Christmas, and thanks."

They watched us leave, and the door thudded closed behind us. We took a couple of paces, and Dehan stopped and poked me in the chest with a woolen finger. She said, "Theresa—"

"Yeah, I know. She told us that she and Lilith were like sisters, but Lilith never shared anything about her boyfriend with her. That struck me as odd at the time."

She nodded. "Yeah, I got that too. But sometimes sisters aren't all that close, right? But this . . . ?"

"They're working in the same hospital, and Theresa is dropping in to pick her up and take her to work. Granted there is no reason to mention it, but odd that she didn't. And there was another comment of Theresa's that struck me. She said she'd report her mother to the cops if she contacted her, because she wasn't fond of her mother, but she was fond of Lilith. I think what we're seeing here, Dehan, is a very close friendship indeed . . . more sisters, like she said. But with a shared reason for keeping it quiet."

She shook her head. "It's not their friendship she's keeping quiet, Stone. It's the boyfriend. She's hiding the boyfriend. That's what she's hiding. You want to go and pull her in?"

I shook my head. "No, not yet. I want a better idea of what the hell is going on before I confront her head-on. I also . . ."

I stopped, thinking, feeling my brain straining. Dehan frowned at me. "What?"

"I want to look at her financials."

"*Lilith's?*"

"Yeah, Lilith's."

"What on Earth for?"

I shrugged, shook my head. "Friday night? People spend money on Friday nights, right . . . ?"

EIGHT

GETTING HOLD OF LILITH'S FINANCIAL RECORDS WAS pretty straightforward because she was the victim of a homicide under investigation. So while I settled down to trawl through her outgoings and income over the year leading up to her death, Dehan phoned Gwen.

"Mrs. Jones, this is Detective Dehan . . . yes, again, good afternoon."

She was quiet for a while. I scanned the pages in front of me, and the first thing that struck me was that Lilith's income of $1,200 per month was paid regularly into her account on the first of every month, from a fund.

Dehan was saying, ". . . just a couple of small details we need to clarify . . ."

I signaled her and showed her a note that read, "Lilith's income where from?"

Dehan gave a single nod. "Lilith had some kind of an income . . . Uh-huh, I see, from a fund left her by her father . . ."

I went back to scanning the pages more minutely. There were random, sporadic outgoings to specialist medical bookstores, Amazon, quite a few to clothes stores, makeup . . . Dehan was saying, "So, did Friday evenings have any special significance for her . . . ?"

Then in June a pattern started to form. It was not strictly every Friday, but most Fridays, there was a payment of twenty-five dollars to Bluebird.

"Work? Just work? Uh-huh, wow, that is real commitment. Sure, Friday and Saturday nights are the worst, drunks, fights, car accidents. Tell me about it, lots of injuries . . ."

I glanced up at her and saw she was arching an eyebrow at me. I turned back to the financials.

By the first week of July, the twenty-five-dollar payments were accompanied by card payments on Friday and Saturday for take-out, and then for cash at ATMs and supermarkets. By the end of the month and the beginning of August she was paying out a minimum of one hundred dollars every Friday and Saturday, twenty-five on the Bluebird, whatever that was, and seventy-five bucks on food and wine.

Dehan hung up. "According to her mother, she had requested to work every Friday and Saturday in the ER to gain experience in emergency treatment of critical injury. That's why she went to the hospital every Friday and didn't come back till late Saturday or Sunday morning."

I slumped back in my chair. "Wherever she was going, Dehan, it wasn't the Harlem Hospital. It was called the Bluebird, and I am guessing it was a motel or a small hotel. By August she was paying out nearly a hundred bucks every Friday and Saturday on food and wine, and a steady twenty-five on this Bluebird."

"So she's meeting her boyfriend at a hotel, and they're having a party every weekend."

"Yeah, that much is obvious. What is less obvious is why Theresa is driving her there. Once you can understand, even twice, but on a regular basis for several months? That makes less sense."

She shook her head. "To you."

"What's that supposed to mean?"

"That you are a black-and-white, straight-down-the-line guy who is very clear about what he wants and what he doesn't want. You want something and you go for it without worrying about what people will think of you or how they'll react. You left all that kind of crap behind when you were . . ." She shrugged and made a face. "I don't know, two?"

"Funny, what are you driving at?"

"To you their behavior seems incomprehensible. But you have to try and remember what it's like to be them: morally uptight, repressed millennials. Lilith was a trainee nurse, and she worked in a charity shop. She hadn't made a life and developed into an adult yet. Millennials don't. She was still living at home with her mom —a mom who was constantly, subtly guilt-tripping her for being beautiful and being a narcissist. Her self-esteem and her self-confidence must have been practically nonexistent."

I grunted. "And her only moral support is Theresa."

"So imagine, Lilith starts an affair with this guy. The way you described her spending, she starts with just sleeping with him, maybe telling herself it will be a one-off and then they'll get married or something. But, surprise, they like it, and they keep meeting. Suddenly this is the highlight of her week, and they are having wine and nice food and they are falling in love with each other." She hesitated. "At least, she is falling in love with him. But, she still hasn't the strength or the resolve to do it alone, so she needs Theresa to take her there. Aside from anything else, it has become part of her cover."

I thought about it and scratched my head. "For six months? You don't think Theresa would reach a point where she'd say, I don't know, 'Get him to pick you up,' 'Find a closer venue,' 'Learn to drive' . . . ?"

"I don't know. We don't really know what Theresa and Lilith's relationship was like. They both had weird families, and they might have clung to each other for support. What we do know is that the Bluebird is probably a hotel, and at that motel there will be somebody who knows who Lilith's boyfriend was."

"Yes, that we do know. Okay, let's see if we can find this place, or at least narrow it down." I pulled over my laptop. "How many Bluebird hotels do you think there are in New York and New Jersey?"

As it turned out there were two: one in West Seneca and one on Long Beach. That was it. There was another in Maine, but logistics and time of travel made Seneca and Maine impossible, which narrowed it down to Long Beach, which was not only feasible, but a depressingly, stereotypically predictable choice.

Dehan pulled her layers of clothing back on, and we made our way out again to the Jag. It wasn't a long drive, but what would normally take less than an hour took us almost an hour and a half, and it was past lunch by the time we finally pulled onto West Broadway and crawled along the vaguely desolate, dispirited winter street of a tawdry holiday resort in the snow.

The Bluebird was a small terrace of two gabled houses with broad porches, which had been knocked into each other to form a small, sad hotel-cum-bed-and-breakfast, one row back from the beach. There were a couple of old cars parked out front that looked as though they had been there since the 1950s. Seven steps formed a stoop to the veranda-cum-porch, and a couple of chipped burgundy flowerpots held a couple of palms that looked like they were surviving but wished they weren't.

We climbed the steps to a glass door with a manically grinning plastic snowman on it. We pushed it open and stepped through into a small reception area with a small flashing Christmas tree that reminded me bizarrely of a meat wagon and a crime scene. There were a couple of chairs by an ancient, imitation-coal electric fire over on the right, and a Formica reception desk on the left. It held a bell and a computer screen, but no receptionist. Dehan hammered on the bell a few times, and a man of about fifty with a large belly and a moth-eaten cardigan emerged through a bead curtain that hung over an arch behind the desk. He was dabbing at his mouth with a napkin.

"'Noon," he said. "Do for ya?"

Clearly he had decided to save time in life by removing the front part of every sentence. I wondered how it was working for him. Perhaps he was a hundred years old and had saved fifty years simply by excising the subject from every verb. Dehan said, "You the manager?"

"'Pends who's askin'. Who's askin'?"

She pulled her badge from her pocket. "Detective Dehan. This is Detective Stone, NYPD."

He nodded at each badge in turn and offered me a smile that was three teeth short of a grin. "Guess I own this joint, then. And I *am* the manager."

I said, "Were you here a year ago?"

"Thirty years 'fore that too."

"Do you remember a young girl, pretty, bright, used to come every Friday and stay till late Saturday, sometimes Sunday . . . ?"

He was nodding before I'd finished. "Sure. Had a name like a flower . . ." He looked up at the ceiling, his face held in a rictus between a grin and thought, while he wrung the napkin in his hands. "Lily, only weren't Lily, was Lilith, Lilith Jones. Lovely kid. Stopped comin'. Always the way. Them things never last."

Dehan asked, "What things?"

He leered at her. "Sexual affairs. People come to small hotels, do things they can't do in their own beds at home. Usually's older people. Get bored with their marriages, need to shake things up a little. Often it's older men with whores or secretaries. Or couples swapping." He laughed. "Comes in Tuesday with his best friend's wife. Then Wednesday best friend comes in with *his* wife! Also see husbands with their boyfriends. Queer, but don't wanna tell their wives. Still get that sometimes. More queers now'n ever before. Never seen that back home when I was a kid. Seen it all here, though. What you don't often see is younger women. Don't happen much." He leaned on the counter, picking at his teeth with his tongue. "Last time Lilith was here was last Christmas, just before. She never come back after that."

"You remember who she came with?"

The sly leer returned to his face, and he eyed Dehan head to foot and back again.

"T'begin with, back in the summer, she come alone. Booked the room on her own, in her own name, with a card. That ain't normal. Turns up, prettiest thing I ever seen, and I'm thinkin', 'She ain't never done this before.' Gets her key and goes to her room, out back, and never shows her face till Saturday night. Never saw who she was with. Figured he was a husband and turned up late and didn't want to be seen."

Dehan sighed. "So did you ever get sight of him or not?"

He shook his head, but he didn't lose the leer. "Thought it was a one-off, but she became a regular. Believe she came just about every Friday for six months. After the second time I was curious, and when she turned up the third time, I saw somebody brung her in a car. Looked like an old Mini Cooper, red."

I cut in. "Did you see the driver?"

He nodded. "Was a woman. Dropped her at the door and drove away. She come in, collected her key like the other times, and went out back to her room."

Dehan sighed noisily. I was reading the leer on his face, and I knew what was coming. Dehan drew breath, but I spoke first.

"You were curious. So you kept an eye out to see who joined her, right?" He shrugged with his eyebrows. I said, "How long did you have to wait till she came back?"

Dehan stared at me. He chuckled. "Half an hour, till dusk. Then I saw the red Mini roll right past and slip into the lot in back. They was trying not to draw too much attention, but they wasn't being real careful either. I looked out the back window, and she parked by the dumpsters, where the car wasn't so visible, and then kind of ran to Lilith's room. They got takeout, and they never come out of that room till Sunday afternoon."

Dehan shook her head. "You're telling us that she was never joined by a man? That her lover was a woman?"

"What I'm telling you, Detective. Same girl who brung her, was the one she was coming to see. Seen just about everything here, and you get plenty a' dykes. But pretty young thing like that? Never seen that before."

"And it was the same for the whole six months?"

"Got bolder, started having regular parties with champagne and wine and music. I don't know why they didn't just get married. They can do that now."

He shrugged. I pulled my cell from my pocket and showed him the picture of Lilith, Ern, and Theresa. He nodded and pointed at Lilith. "That's Lilith right there, and that"—he indicated Theresa—"that's her girlfriend." Now he frowned at me. "What they done?"

I sighed. "I don't know. Did anybody ever come asking about them?" He shook his head. "Did anybody visit them, turn up unexpectedly. Did you ever get the impression they were being watched? Did anybody show any interest in them at all? Was there ever an incident, anything . . . ?"

He shook his head throughout.

"Nothing. Nothing like that. Turned up, had their weekends, and left. Always left it clean and tidy, never caused problems, and nobody ever turned up looking for them. Not till now."

I scrolled through my phone and found the photograph of Pat, showed it to him. "This woman ever show up? You ever seen her?"

He made a face and shook his head. "Never seen that woman before in my life. She's butt ugly. I'd remember if I had. Who the hell is she?"

We left him peering out the window at us as we made our way carefully down the stoop to the Jag. When we got to the bottom, Dehan said, "I need to drive," and held out a woolen hand. I gave her the keys, stuffed my hands in my pockets, and leaned against the car.

"Is it relevant?"

She stopped halfway 'round the hood and glanced at me. Then continued on 'round to open the door. "That I want to drive?"

"You're being facetious."

"I have a right. I am cold and confused."

She climbed in, and I got in beside her. We slammed the doors in unison, and she fumbled with the key, trying to fit it in the ignition with woolen hands.

"Is it relevant that Lilith was gay? Is it relevant that she and Theresa were lovers?"

The key slipped in. She turned it, and the big old engine roared, then rumbled, idling while she stared out the windshield. I said, "Ninety percent of murders are about sex, so yeah, I guess it's relevant. Why wouldn't it be?"

She put it in first and pulled away. "Where are we going?"

"First right, five blocks to Park Avenue, then left and stop outside the Brixx and Barley, brick oven pizzas and tap brews."

"See? That's why I married you."

"That, my sculpted body, and my fine chiseled features." I took a deep breath and added, "We need to remember that she was stabbed in the back with Pat's scissors, Dehan."

"Point?"

"On the face of it, Pat's scissors have nothing to do with Lilith being gay, or having an affair with Theresa."

She stared at me with a deeply skeptical face. "No? How about if she'd just found out that Lilith had corrupted her daughter and turned her into a lesbian?"

I stared out at the listless, cold buildings and the empty streets drifting by, frosted by icy, North Atlantic winds; I thought about the warm, toasted promise of the thin, crispy pizza, a nut-brown IPA, and maybe a Bushmills to round it off afterward, given that Dehan felt the need to drive.

Setting those thoughts aside, I tried to visualize Pat Perkins alone in her Christmas house, Cyril on his way to take Ern home, Theresa at home with her husband and child, Lilith hurrying home after two or three hours with Mrs. Rodriguez on the corner of Gildersleeve, and Gwen Jones waiting at home for her daughter to arrive.

What happened? Theresa picked that moment to call her mother and tell her she had a lesbian lover? Pat phoned her, and what started as a Christmas greeting escalated into an argument in which Theresa confessed she had become gay . . . ? None of the scenarios I came up with rang particularly true.

We came to Park Avenue, and Dehan swung the wheel left.

"You know what, Dehan? If Pat discovered that Theresa was having a lesbian affair with Lilith, I don't honestly think she would give a damn." I turned to look at her. "I think Theresa barely existed for Pat. Pat was only interested in men, and controlling them. The only women she was aware of were the ones who constituted a threat."

NINE

THE CALL CAME AS I WAS CUTTING INTO MY PIZZA. I sighed, laid down my knife, picked up my cell, and said, "Stone," into the receiver.

"Detective, this is Officer Maria Vazquez. I've been checking your list of Robert Hansens . . ."

"Yes, Vazquez, any luck?"

"Detective, I found a Robert Hansen, aka Bobby Hansen, in San Diego.""Okay."

"But when I called, it was his ex-wife, Felicia, who answered. It turned out he'd moved about a year ago."

"Where'd he move to?"

"He'd moved east, to Philly. She didn't seem to like him too much and was happy to give me his number and his address. She said it hadn't been hard for her to track him down through mutual friends. She said he makes his money selling dope, especially crystal meth, and that's what took him to Philly."

"Okay, Vazquez, good work. Did you ask her about Pat Perkins?"

"So, I asked her if she knew whether he'd ever been involved with one Patricia Perkins née Hartwell, and she went nuts."

"Nuts how?"

"She called her a crazy bitch and a—excuse me, Detective—quote, 'fucking psycho.' I didn't go into it any further, Detective, because I thought you'd want me to contact you straightaway. It seems to be our man."

"Good work, Vazquez. Give me his address and number."

"Five fifty, East Indiana Avenue, in Philly." She followed that with a telephone number and hung up.

I took a bite of my pizza and spoke around it. "We have Robert Hansen."

"We do?"

"He's living in the Philly Badlands."

"That's two hours on the I-95."

I nodded. "But there's the small matter of jurisdiction. The Twenty-Fourth District don't take too kindly to people nosing around their turf. Mostly because their turf is full of . . ."

"Yeah, language, Detective Stone. However, what you say is true. What do you suggest?"

"I suggest an unofficial visit in which we suggest to Mr. Hansen that if he doesn't cooperate and tell us what we want to know, we'll bundle him in the trunk and take him back to San Diego where his ex is more than willing to testify against him and put him away for ten to fifteen years."

"That would be illegal, Stone."

"Which is why I would never do it. Say, I have an aunt who lives in or near Philly, and I keep meaning to drop in and visit her."

"Yeah? What's her address?"

"That's the thing, I don't recall exactly. It might have been five fifty, East Indiana Avenue."

"Isn't that right in the heart of the Badlands?"

"You're right. And with Christmas coming up, she must be feeling really sad and alone. We should visit."

Dehan drained her beer, folded what was left of her pizza into her mouth, and stood. "C'mong, Shtome. Lesh go bijit yom aunch. Sh'Quishmash fr crying ouchlow!"

I sighed and stood. "All the way to Philly now? Hell, Dehan, you have no mercy."

"Nong," she said, swallowing and pulling on her coat.

"None at all," I agreed.

Dehan's estimate of two hours proved to be optimistic, based as it was on good weather conditions and traffic. But with the freezing temperatures, black ice, and slow-moving vehicles, we didn't hit Philly till six that evening, when we caught the tail end of the rush hour. Then we crawled through cold, ugly streets lined with dilapidated squats, grim shop fronts with peeling paint and window displays of Santas, reindeer, and snowmen, protected behind steel mesh. We finally pulled up outside 550 East Indiana Avenue at almost seven p.m. It was a dilapidated, two-story redbrick, where the red bricks had turned to a dirty brown.

There was a flat, peeling blue door and what looked like blankets hanging over the inside of the windows. I hammered on the plywood door, and one of the sash windows upstairs slid open and a drawn, pasty face leaned out. It was hard to tell in the failing light if it was a man or a woman, but the voice proved to be a woman's.

"What d'you want? He ain't in. If you're looking for Bobby, he ain't here."

"Where is he? We're friends of his. We brought some stuff for him he wanted us to collect."

She hesitated. "I don't think I should tell you. You look like cops."

I glanced at Dehan, and we both laughed. I looked up at her worried face. "He won't thank you for not telling us, but if it helps, I can let you have twenty for the information."

"Make it thirty."

"Make it thirty then. Where is he?"

The window slid closed, and after a moment we heard heavy feet on the stairs. Then the door opened a few inches and a skeletal woman with sunken cheeks and peroxide hair peered out.

"Where's the money?"

I pulled out my wallet and took out thirty bucks. "Where's Bobby?"

"At the sports bar two blocks up, corner of Rorer Street. That's where he hangs out, you know, does business. I keep the place for him." She glanced from me to Dehan and back. "Used to do a bit of whoring, make some dough, but I ain't got the looks no more."

"That's too bad. Speaking of looks, what's he like?"

"You're friends and you don't know what he looks like?"

"Yeah, friendship can be funny like that. What does he look like?"

She shrugged. "Forty-something, tall, skinny, curly red hair and . . ." She waggled her fingertips over her cheeks and nose. "Freckles on his face. Jeans and a black Snoopy sweatshirt. And a big brown coat. Like wool."

I nodded. "You got somebody watching your health?"

She stared at me a moment, then screwed up her face and her eyes. "Go fuck yourself. Fuck you. Go fuck yourself, asshole!"

"Sure, you have a nice day."

We turned and made our way up the road on foot, pulling our coats tight about our bodies against the icy blades of the wind. Behind us we could hear the screech of her voice, screaming she didn't need nobody watching her goddamned health. She didn't need nothing. The last shout was carried away on the freezing air, but I just made out the words, "*Tell Bobby I got some cash. Tell him to hurry home!*"

The sports bar was the Slam Dunk. It was an ugly, pseudo-Georgian building in soiled beige with Grecian columns holding up an Arcadian pediment over a plate glass door. A fluorescent sign in the window said they served Budweiser beer. Another said they showed sports all day.

I looked at Dehan and growled, "Stay behind me and let me do the talking."

She snorted a cloud of condensation and muttered something that sounded like "Dork!"

I pushed through the door into the warm noise of loud conversation and TV commentators following a game of football. The smell was predominantly wet coats and stale beer, but there was also that hint of singed cabbage that tells you somebody is smoking dope. We made our way to the bar where a guy with a face like a hunk of rubble jerked his chin at me and ignored Dehan. I leaned my elbows on the bar and said, "Gimme two beers."

He cracked two bottles and put them in front of me. I handed one to Dehan, and we turned to survey the room. It didn't take long to find Hansen. He was exactly as his neighbor had described him, and he was sitting in the corner, under the TV, reading the *New York Times*.

I touched Dehan's arm, and we crossed the wooden floor to his table. He looked up as we approached, and his eyes told me he knew we were cops. I spoke as I pulled out a chair.

"Mind if we join you?"

He nodded. "Yeah, I do. Who are you?"

I smiled at him all over my right cheek. "I'm the meanest son of a bitch in the valley, and this is my partner, Tinker Bell. And you, well, you're Bobby Hansen, from Southern Cali. You've got that beach boy look." I turned my smile to Dehan, who had pulled her woolly hat off and was stuffing it in her pocket. "Don't he have that beach boy look, Tink?"

She gave me a baleful look, which she then turned on Hansen. Her voice, when it came, was dead. "Yeah, all sun, sand, and sea."

"You're funny. You should do an act. What do you want?"

I said, "We just dropped by to say hello. Oh, and Felicia sends her very best regards."

Dehan chuckled. It was an unsettling sound. "She says she's bought a special wooden box inlaid with ivory and mother-of-pearl. She says that's where she plans to keep your nuts after she's laid her hands on you."

I allowed myself a small laugh. "She sounds like a real funny lady. Did you know she's been talking to the LAPD about you?

They all seem to think you're a real interesting guy. Just about everybody out there wants to talk to you."

Dehan spoke in her dead voice again. "It's moving. Emotionally moving. We thought, with such an outpouring of feeling, what we really wanted to do more than anything else, Bob, was take you back to your wife, so all your friends could gather around and be with you."

His eyes narrowed. You could feel the tension humming around him. "You're not LAPD. You don't look like LAPD. You bounty hunters? Who the hell are you?"

I said, "I told you. We're friends of Felicia's. She really wants you to come home, Bobby. She misses you real bad."

"Like hell."

I stopped smiling, and we both gave him the dead eye. I said, "I got the car right outside, full tank. We're ready to go."

His face drained of all color. His eyes became wide and shifted from my face to behind me, searching for someone. Dehan flashed me a small smile and shifted in her chair. Hansen said, "You can't take me back. I ain't going back. You don't understand. She don't get it." He shook his head. "No, if I go back . . ." Again he shook his head. "I owe money. To real bad people."

I showed my teeth in an ugly grin. "Real bad people? Worse than us?"

"Listen, I owe money to the Tijuana cartel, man. You don't understand that. I *can't* go back. *You* know what they'll do to me! *Come on!*"

I'd been watching Dehan's face. She'd been watching something going on behind me, and now her eyes rose to stare up into a face just in back of my right shoulder. There was amusement in her eyes. I felt less amused when her eyes moved to a presence in back of my left shoulder too. Hansen's face, on the other hand, registered relief.

A voice like Barry White with a hangover said, "You okay, bro? You look unhappy."

Dehan, looking like a large sack of merino wool, stood. I

stood too and turned. There were two big black guys. Each was easily six three or four, and two hundred and sixty pounds of solid muscle. The guy on my left, who was now smiling down at Dehan, was as bald as an eight ball. The one looking down at me had tight braids all over his head and an ugly scar down his cheek that twisted his mouth into a sneer. He shook his head at me. "Oh, man, you really don't wanna stand up."

Before I could answer, the bald guy had unleashed his deep bass rumble again, leering at Dehan. "Binky, you know what I found me here?"

The guy with the braids was still staring into my eyes. He said, "Whatshou found, bro?"

"I found me a piece of tasty brown meat. I think I'm gonna take me this meat into the can and eat it right now."

Binky didn't shift his gaze, but he grinned. "Yeah? Well, you leave some for me, Roy. I want some o' that brown meat for me too."

In my peripheral vision I saw Bobby Hansen get to his feet. Roy growled, "You better get outta here, Bobby. Things about to get real ugly."

Dehan moved with the speed of a snake. From her standing position she lashed out in a blinding side kick that was half kick and half stamp and smashed her heel into the side of Roy's right knee. There was a nauseating *clack*, and the noise that came out of his mouth made the hair on the back of my neck stand up. It was like a high-pitched wail of disbelief as his leg bent into a horrifically unnatural shape. But he had little time to contemplate that gruesome shape because Dehan's woolly elbow had smashed sickeningly into the tip of his jaw and he crumpled to the floor, sending a chair spinning.

I didn't give Binky time to register what had happened. While his mouth was open, gaping at his fallen pal, I stepped in and drove a right cross into the tip of his jaw. I heard the joint crack, his eyes rolled up in his head, and he went over backward like a felled tree, and he hit the wooden floor like a sack of cement.

The bar had fallen silent; aside from the frantic babble of the TV sports commentators, there was only a very dangerous hush. Dehan stepped over to Bobby, who stood frozen in his tracks. She grabbed a handful of the back of his head and whispered in his ear. Then we started to move toward the door. I shifted my jacket so the butt of my Sig Sauer P226 was visible and spoke loudly to the rubble-faced barman.

"Those two men had a fight. One of them broke the other's knee, and got his jaw broken in that same, unfortunate exchange of blows. I think, barman, that you would be well advised to notify an ambulance. A good evening to you all."

With that I opened the door, and we stepped outside into the freezing evening. There Bobby started hissing condensation as between us we took his elbows and bustled him toward his house.

"What have you *done*? Do you know what you have *done*? Holy shit, man! That was Roy Scooter and Binky James, man! You broke his *leg*! Oh man! *Oh man!*"

Dehan said mildly, "Shut up. Do as you're told and you'll be okay."

"Oh man . . ."

I said, "Give me your key."

He stared at me as though I'd given him some really bad news he couldn't quite believe. "What . . . ?"

"Give-me-your-key. Now. Your key. Give it to me."

He made a "wha" sound a few times, fumbled in his pocket, and pulled out a key ring. I took it from his hands as we arrived at the Jag. Then I stepped ahead and unlocked the door.

We bustled straight into a small, dark living room. I snapped on the light and saw a couple of collapsed sofas covered in Mexican-patterned blankets and an old, glass-topped coffee table. On it there was a small box shaped like an old pirate's chest and beside that a glass ashtray with a few pieces of screwed-up tinfoil and a pipe.

Dehan gave Bobby a small shove, and he stumbled a couple of paces. I said, "Sit down, Robert," and Dehan closed the door behind her and leaned against it. He lowered himself onto the far sofa and watched us.

I said to her, "Do you know what the penalty is for possession of marijuana in Pennsylvania, Mrs. Smith?"

"As a second offense, about three years, Mr. Brown. But, given the tenant upstairs, I'm willing to bet he's got more than marijuana sitting around in this house."

I nodded and gave a small laugh. "That's right. We gave her thirty bucks to tell us where you were. She wanted us to give you a message to hurry home. I think she wanted to buy something from you. What do you say, Bobby, shall we call her down, see what it is she wants to buy?"

He didn't answer. He just stared at us with large, terrified eyes. I turned to Dehan again.

"I tell you what, Mrs. Smith. I think we are lacking in ambition. Let us not forget that this man has crossed an entire continent. He has come from Southern California, where certain Mexican gentlemen of the knife-wielding persuasion are keen to get their hands on him, not to mention their blades. What we seem to have here is drug trafficking not just across state borders, but across international borders. I think perhaps we should be calling Bernie at the bureau."

His face, at first just ghostly, now turned a whiter shade of pale. "Come on, man. It's just a bit of dope. Everybody does it. I'm not into anything big-time. I'm small-time. What the hell do you want with me . . . ?"

"Nothing big-time, except that you have the Tijuana cartel hunting for you, out for your blood. You really don't want one of their *sicarios* to find you, Bobby. I think your safest bet is the Feds."

"Please don't do this, man. Please. You're killing me."

Dehan snorted. "Sounds like you took care of that yourself, pal. You're already one of the living dead."

"Who the hell *are* you? If you're cops, why don't you just say so? Come *on*, man!"

I pulled my cell from my pocket. "We're nobody, Bobby. We were never here, and you never saw us. The Feds will come and take care of you. We will be gone."

"No, come on, please, you guys . . ."

"Unless . . ."

It was Dehan. He turned to her, despair, hope, and gratitude alive in his eyes.

"Unless? Unless what? Anything, man, just tell me. What do you want?"

I sat on the sofa opposite him and leaned my elbows on my knees. "Tell us," I said, "about Pat."

He frowned at me like I was crazy. "*Pat?*"

I nodded. "Pat. Patricia Hartwell, later Perkins."

His jaw sagged. "Patty? You want to know about *Patty?*" He began to laugh. "What the hell for?"

I pulled my cell from my pocket again and made like I was dialing. What I did was start to record. Bobby stopped laughing and held out both hands toward me. "Okay, wait. Wait! Stop that. I'll tell you. I just don't know what the hell you wanna know about Pat."

I set the phone on the table and said quietly, "You are Robert Hansen, right?"

"Yeah, of course."

"And you know Patricia Perkins, née Hartwell?"

He swallowed. "You know I do."

"So, Bobby, I want to know where she is."

TEN

He stared at Dehan for a long moment, then at me. He swallowed and shook his head.

"I don't know. She married some guy in New York."

Dehan spoke from over by the door. "But you stayed in touch."

He made a weeping face and spread his hands. "It was a holiday thing. We played around for a couple of weeks. She wasn't so big back then, but I like big women anyway. You know? It was fun. She went back to New York. We used to send each other dirty messages for a laugh, and once a year she'd go west for a holiday. We'd screw around for a couple of weeks. Then she'd go home.

"One year she sends me a message." He laughed. "The stupid bitch is apologizing because she never told me she was married. Like I give a shit, man! I told her I would never forget her and I was gonna go blow my fuckin' brains out. It was *sarcasm, man!*" He leaned forward, staring at Dehan like he thought she was a moron, shaking his head. "*Sarcasm!* You know it? It's spelt S-A-R-C-A-S-M! Well, the stupid *fuckin'* bitch thought I was serious, for crying out loud! And she starts sending me messages like she didn't realize I cared so much. She thought it was just a holiday affair. If only she had known. You know? Like we just found each other. Fuckin' soul mates. That kind of crap.

"I was gonna tell her she was out of her fuckin' mind, but she showed up next summer and, man, the sex was crazy. She was wild. You know what I'm saying? She was on a mission. She was telling me she was gonna divorce this dude and move out west. And, man, I'm telling you, as long as she was doing what she was doing, I was *not* going to burst her bubble."

He started to laugh again. "So I thought, if she is this crazy normally, what the hell is she gonna be like if she gets high, man? So I convinced her to smoke some weed. Dude!" He screamed with laughter. "*Dude!* She was *wild*! I am tellin' you, W-I-L-D! We broke the fuckin' bed! And next thing she is talking about is how she's gonna fuckin' kill her husband! *Kill her fuckin' husband!* And I'm like, *what*? I'm like *fuckin' what?*"

Dehan came and sat beside me. "Kill her husband? Did she say how?"

He waved both hands at her. "No, man, it's worse than that. She is tellin' me she's gonna kill her husband *and her daughter.*"

I held up a hand. "Wait a minute! Wait a minute! How long ago did this happen?"

"Like, I don't know. Two years ago?"

"She said she was going to kill her husband and her daughter two years ago?"

"Yeah, man. But like, when she said that I broke off with her. That was too crazy for me. I didn't want to know. I know women have hormones and get depression and that kind of crazy shit. So I'm thinking, next thing she's gonna want to kill me, right?"

"What happened after that?"

"Nothing happened."

I sighed. "Come on, Bobby. You want to be helping us here, remember? What exactly is nothing? What happened?"

"She went back to New York. When she was gone I wrote her and told her I was getting married. I was already married but she didn't know that. So I told her I couldn't see her no more and to do her best to forget me."

Dehan sniffed. "Forget you? Like that would be hard."

"Hey! She loved me, man."

I cut him short. "How did she react?"

He puffed out his cheeks and blew loudly. "It was complicated. She was real mad. I mean *real* mad. She was kind of possessive, territorial, jealous. So she went pretty nuts. She said she was gonna find my fiancée and kill her. For a bit she was saying she was gonna kill me too. I got her to chill a bit and agreed that we could still meet during her holidays. But I'm telling you, she was crazy, man. She understood things the way she wanted to understand them. Next thing she's telling me we're in love and she's gonna move out west and we're gonna live together . . ." He shook his head. "It was intense, man."

Dehan said, "So what happened?"

"I kept telling her to chill, to take it easy. At least she stopped talking about killing people. Then, last Christmas, she just went off the radar."

I stared down at the grimy carpet between my feet. "Off the radar, huh?"

"Yeah man, just kind of stopped."

"And you have no idea why."

"No, man."

I nodded a few times, thinking, then said, "Okay, Bobby, you have a choice here. You can come with us, or you can stay here."

I looked him in the eye and held it. He frowned, drew breath, and went to speak, then stopped. Then realization began to dawn. "If I stay . . ."

I nodded. Dehan said, "There's no telling who will show up looking for you, Bobby. You've been very careless, and careless people are easy to track. Look at us!"

"So where are you going to take me?"

I said, "Somewhere safe. We need you as a material witness."

"To what?"

"Murder."

He went pasty and waxy again. "Who . . . ? What murder? I ain't witness to no murder."

Dehan stood. "Pat Perkins didn't kill her husband and her daughter. Lucky for them they were out of the house when she finally went crazy. But she killed her next-door neighbor."

"Holy shit. How am I a witness to that?"

I stood. "That is a very good question, Bobby, and one I mean to answer very soon. Pack whatever you need and get in the car."

He stared at us a moment, doing some rapid calculations in his head. Finally he said, "You're New York cops."

I nodded and pointed at his front door. "With no jurisdiction here. Which means that if the next people to walk through that door are Badlands cops doing their Mexican friends a favor, or the Feds, or anybody else with a grudge against you, we will have no jurisdiction to help you. So right now your safest option is to get to New York as soon as you can. Because we must be among the very few people on this planet who actually want you alive. We're going that way, so if you want a ride, pack a suitcase and let's go."

He thought about it a second longer, then went next door to pack a bag. When he'd closed the door, Dehan frowned at me and spoke quietly.

"You think he's hiding her? I think he's telling the truth."

"I think you're right."

"So . . . ?"

I nodded. "Exactly."

She scowled. "Stone!"

"You know what the hardest thing to prove is, Ritoo Glasshopper?"

"I know you're going to tell me."

"A negative." I pointed at the bedroom door. "This guy can prove it for us."

"But, prove what? That . . . ?"

The door opened, and he came out holding a sports bag.

"Okay, I'm ready." He hesitated, looking vaguely nauseated. "Am I walking into a trap? Are you going to arrest me? Or kill me?"

"For the last time, we are out of our jurisdiction, Bobby. We're just offering you a ride to New York, where you're going to help the police with their inquiries. What you do after that is up to you, but I'd recommend cutting a deal with the Feds to get your Mexican friends off your back."

"Oh . . ." He nodded a few times. "Oh, okay, let's go then."

———

TWO HOURS later Bobby Hansen was in an interrogation room at the 43rd and Dehan and I were in the chief's office. His expression, usually affable and courteous to a fault, was strained.

"John . . ." He sighed and ran his fingers through his thick, salt-and-pepper hair. "John," he said again in a descending tone that said his patience was running dry and he blamed me. "You're explaining it to me, and yet I don't understand. Exactly how is this man, Robert Hansen, whom you have, effectively, kidnapped from Pennsylvania, a material witness in the Perkins case?"

Dehan half stood and sat again. "Oh, he came entirely voluntarily, sir. He asked us for a ride."

He looked at her a moment through hooded eyes, then turned to me. "John?"

I took a big lungful of air, held my breath for a count of three, and let it out in a long puff.

"It is not easy, sir. Please bear with me. Here's the thing . . ."

"Explain the thing, John. I am very curious to hear what the thing is."

"The assumption has been, from the start, that Pat Perkins managed somehow to vanish without leaving a trace."

He arched an eyebrow at me. "That seems a fair assumption seeing as that is, in fact, exactly what she has done."

"Yes, sir. But there has always been a big question mark over her disappearance. How could a woman of limited intelligence and zero skill in the field achieve such a complete disappearance? It's a feat spooks, terrorists, experts in the field struggle to achieve. Yet she pulled it off without apparently trying. Even if she had left the country, she would have left some kind of trace."

He shrugged. "Unless she was one of the millions who cross into Mexico every day without showing their passport."

"That is possible, sir, but it doesn't make a lot of sense."

"No?"

"No, sir. We have found no connection with Mexico at all. She made no money out of this killing, and she did not clean out her account. Unless she had been stashing money away over the years, she left with what she had in her purse, and she didn't use her credit or debit cards after she left. A woman like Pat, not a skilled criminal or a spook, would be lost in Mexico with no money. The same reasoning applies to Canada. Besides, there was a BOLO out that night for her and her car. She would have been spotted."

He grunted. "All right, John, I see what you mean, but it still doesn't explain why you have brought this man in on what are essentially false pretenses."

"Okay, baby steps, sir. My starting point was that it was not feasible that Pat could have disappeared like that without help from somebody. Somebody who knows how to disappear, somebody with some experience of criminal activity, or at least fieldcraft. When we stumbled across Bobby Hansen, he seemed to fit the bill as a coconspirator, at least to some extent, especially when he told us Pat had talked about killing her husband and her daughter. But now it's clear to both of us, sir, that he does not fit the bill at all. In fact, he stopped hearing from Pat the very Christmas she died."

"Perhaps he's lying."

Dehan shook her head. "If he is, he's the best damn liar I've ever seen. And besides, what's he doing in a slum in Philly if he's hooked up with Pat in California?"

"There is one other point, sir. Hansen's flight from California was extremely incompetent. He was easy to track, and half the reason I brought him in was to save his life, because he had a Mexican cartel on his heels. But Pat's disappearance was engineered by an expert. Hansen is anything but an expert."

"All right." He shook his head and spread his hands. "So what was the other half of the reason?"

I sagged back in my chair and drummed my palms on the arms. "Because I need to prove a negative. Sir, I have not let you down yet, and I am going to ask for your tolerance and your lenience here. What I want to do is highly unconventional, but I sincerely believe it is the only way to crack this case."

"What are you talking about, John?"

"I need Bobby Hansen alive, because I need to prove what didn't happen."

Dehan screwed up her eyes and turned to stare at me. The inspector looked at me as though I had spouted word salad at him. "You need to do *what*?"

"I can't explain it right now, sir. All I can say is that this case is all about what didn't happen. Pat Perkins did not go to California with Bobby Hansen, and Bobby Hansen did not help her to disappear. I need to be able to prove that."

He shook his head. "We can't charge him with anything. Plus, you brought him in as a material witness! A material witness to what *didn't* happen?"

Dehan stared at me a moment, then turned to the chief. "Sir, I think Stone has taken leave of his senses. To me it is plainly obvious that Pat went to this man in California, as they had both arranged for her to do the summer before, and he is now concealing her. If she killed Lilith, as all the forensic evidence seems to suggest, then he is giving her succor and is therefore an accomplice. He is, then, as Stone said, a material witness."

I suppressed a smile. The inspector wagged a finger at her, sighed, and wagged his finger again. "You two are brilliant, but one day, *one day*, you will overstep the line and then you will cause me no end of trouble! But this had better not lead to lawsuits and claims for compensation for abuse of power!"

We stood, and I showed the chief my phone. "There is nowhere on Earth Hansen would rather be right now than in a prison surrounded by armed cops. And even if he complains, we have enough on this recording to send him back to Philly and have him put away for a long stretch. He will cooperate with us, sir."

He sighed again. "He'd better, John. He'd better. What is your next move?"

"I want to leave Hansen meditating about his future for a bit, sir, and before we go any further with him, I want to talk to Theresa Perkins again."

"Oh? Why?"

He leaned back and frowned. Dehan answered. "It looks as though Theresa and Lilith were actually having a lesbian affair, sir. If Theresa concealed that, she may have concealed other things too. Lilith claimed to have spent a long time with her elderly neighbor the night she was killed, more than seems likely. We think she may have been with Theresa." She hesitated a moment. "There is something—a person or an event—connecting Lilith and Theresa on the one side and Pat and possibly Hansen on the other. It's there, that night, when Lilith was killed and Pat got in her car and drove away. We just can't make out what it is yet."

We stepped out of the chief's office and walked slowly down the stairs to the detectives' room and our desk. All the way I was thinking about what Dehan had said, and suddenly everything made sense.

I sat and pulled my pen from my pocket. I found a scrap of paper and scrawled something on it. Then I slipped the paper in an envelope, sealed it, and handed it to Dehan.

"That"—I wagged the pen at the envelope—"is the answer to the case. I can't prove it yet, so there is no point reading it. When we close the case, open that envelope. If I am right, you owe me a week in Hawaii. If I am wrong, I will do whatever you want for a week."

"Jerk."

"That's all you have to say?"

"Yeah. Oh, and also, I guess you are taking me to Hawaii."

I gave her my smuggest grin. "You want to call Theresa, or shall I?"

"I'll call. You drive." She shouldered on her coat and pulled on her hat. "Tonight I want pizza, wine, and old black-and-white movies. And a foot massage."

I stood and followed her woolen form toward the door. "Your wish is my command," I said, and meant it.

ELEVEN

THERESA AGREED TO COME INTO THE STATION AT TEN thirty the next morning. So we had a leisurely breakfast of bacon and eggs and arrived at the station at twenty past, in time for Dehan to get three cups of coffee from the corner deli while I parked the burgundy beast among what was left of the melting drifts outside the 43rd.

The sky was a sharp ice blue, and the Atlantic wind was laced with invisible scalpels. I stood at the entrance to the station, stamping and puffing while Dehan, looking like the Queen of the Yeti, approached carrying three large coffees. I took one from her, and we climbed the stairs to the interrogation room in silence.

Theresa watched us walk in, and you could see the fear in her eyes. Dehan put the coffee on the table and began to pull off her layers of wool.

I said, "Good morning, Theresa." She nodded, watching me. I smiled. "Thanks for coming in."

"What's this about?"

Dehan cleared her throat and placed her hat and gloves on the table.

"You know what it's about, Theresa." Theresa didn't say

anything, and Dehan went on. "It's about your mother, and where she is."

"I already told you all I know about that."

Dehan screwed up her nose and made a kind of "Nyeh!" noise, followed by a "Tsk!" and "But you didn't really, did you?"

"What do you mean? What are you talking about?"

I sat next to Dehan and regarded Theresa for a moment. I tried a long shot, just to see where it would land.

"We know, Theresa."

She went slightly pale and pulled back in her chair. When she spoke, her throat was constricted and her voice came out like a dry croak.

"You know what? What are you talking about?"

"About Lilith, Theresa. We know about Lilith."

"Lilith . . . ?"

Dehan sighed. "Why don't you tell us about it, Theresa. More to the point, why *didn't* you tell us about it?"

She gave her head small shakes. "You're fishing."

I smiled. "You and Lilith were lovers, Theresa. We know about the Bluebird. How could you have thought we wouldn't find out?"

She leaned forward on the table and buried her face in her hands. "Oh God . . . Oh dear God."

Dehan spoke quietly. "Your husband doesn't know?"

Theresa shook her head. "We were engaged at the time."

"How did Lilith feel about that?"

She dragged her hands down her face and looked over her fingers at Dehan.

"At first it was a . . ." She paused, shook her head, and shrugged. "It was just a crazy adventure, an escapade. This is so humiliating!"

I sipped my coffee. Dehan said, "Believe me, we have heard much, much worse."

"Billy, that's my husband, confessed to me once that he liked to fantasize that Lilith and me . . ." She spread her hands. ". . . had a *thing* going on. It had never crossed my mind. I thought it was crazy and it made me kind of mad. I told Lilith and . . ." She stopped and drew breath. "I thought she'd be indignant, or laugh, but, well, she hit me with this bombshell. She said she had always had a crush on me, and, well . . ."

Dehan put in the missing words: "She was open to having an affair with you."

"At first I was horrified. I didn't talk to her for a couple of days, but I couldn't stop thinking about it. In the end she called me. She was so upset and thought she had lost me as a friend. We met, got drunk, and I ended up letting her kiss me."

I said, "That was when she booked the hotel room?"

She heaved a big sigh. "This is very difficult for me. I am not a lesbian. It was just her, then . . . I don't know how to explain it."

"We are not here to judge you, Theresa. We only want to understand what happened."

"We decided—*I* decided—we needed to get it out of our systems and move on, as though nothing had happened." She sighed again. "That was the plan. My plan."

Dehan said, "But it didn't work out that way."

"You could say that. We . . . the connection, the chemistry, whatever you want to call it, was so powerful. We could hardly wait to be together. It became a nightmare, but it was heaven as well."

I scratched my head. "Why didn't you tell your fiancé?"

"Because . . ." Her face flushed red, and tears sprang into her eyes. "Because I wasn't *in love* with her! I told you! I am *not* a lesbian! I was in love with Bill, but the fascination with Lilith was overpowering."

I drummed my fingers on the table, exploring the angles with my mind. "Did she feel the same way?"

She didn't answer. She sat staring at the edge of the table. Dehan prompted her.

"Was it just a fascination for Lilith?"

Theresa shook her head. "No. I should have stopped it when I saw the signs, but I couldn't."

"She started to fall in love with you." I leaned forward on my elbows. "Or was she always in love with you, from the start?"

"I came to realize that, too late."

"So when she supposedly spent three hours with Mrs. Rodriguez on Christmas evening, she was really with you."

She closed her eyes, and her skin went like wax, the pouches under her eyes a sickly blue. For a moment I thought she would pass out, but she nodded.

"Yes, I was with her just before . . ."

I cut in, "Tell us what happened, Theresa."

"We had prearranged it with Mrs. Rodriguez, who thought we were going to see our boyfriends. She thought it was a great gas. I was at Mrs. Rodriguez's house when Lilith arrived, and I took Lilith to my apartment on Patterson Avenue. Bill thought I was working. We spent a couple of hours together, and I took her home. That is, I dropped her at Mrs. Rodriguez's house."

Dehan asked, "How were things between you?"

"Tense. She had steadily progressed from—" She stopped, mustered her strength, and said, "*Sex!* I'm sorry if that sounds brutal, but that is what it was for me! And I thought that was what it was for her to start with, but she progressed to wanting candlelit dinners, wine, flowers . . . At first it was fun, but it became more and more serious with her, and I didn't know how to get out of it. That last day was difficult, very difficult."

I said, "What was it that made it so difficult?"

"She wanted me to leave Bill." She gave a small laugh. "I wasn't going to leave Bill! I loved Bill!"

"Did you tell her that?"

"Yes! Of course I did."

"How did she take that?"

"Not well."

We waited. Finally Dehan pressed her. "How? What did she do?"

"She cried a lot. She said I had used her, that I had played with her. She did everything from rage to moral blackmail. In the end I promised her we would talk things over and I wouldn't make any hasty decisions. But we both knew that all my decisions were already made."

We sat in silence for a while, she watching her hands on the edge of the table, Dehan and I watching her. Finally Dehan asked, "Was it only moral blackmail that she used?"

She didn't look up. "What do you mean?"

"Didn't she threaten to talk to Bill?"

She swallowed and moved her mouth a few times before saying, "No. Lilith would not have sunk that low."

I smiled and looked down at the tabletop. "Do you know how many years of experience Detective Dehan and I have between us?" She didn't say anything. I went on, "Over fifty. Do you know how many interrogations that translates to? I don't, but it must be thousands. And if there is one thing we have both learned, Theresa, it's that the noblest, most honorable people will sink just as low as the rest of us when they are in love, and in fear of losing the person they love. We can all sink that low if the conditions are right."

"All right." She shrugged. "What's the use. She did. She said she would tell Bill. I was cruel. I laughed and told her he would be delighted. It was his idea in the first place."

"Is that true?" It was Dehan. "Would he have been delighted?"

"No. Most people are surprisingly terrified of seeing their fantasies become reality. Reality has a way of turning dreams sour."

I leaned back in my chair, thinking. Dehan pressed her further. "I guess that depends on the dream, Theresa. But there is something I am not clear about."

Theresa glanced at her. Maybe it was something indefinable in Dehan's voice, but she looked scared. "What?"

"The scissors."

Theresa frowned. "What?"

"How did you get the scissors?"

"*What . . . ?*" She stared at me, then back at Dehan. "The *scissors*? My mother's scissors? You think *I* . . ." She laughed. "You must be out of your mind!"

Dehan snapped, "Really? Why? You had motive and opportunity. She was about to destroy your future marriage. She might even have destroyed your career. Your whole life. You already said you weren't in love with her, that it was just sex. You had every reason to kill her. What I don't get is how you got hold of the scissors."

She was shaking her head throughout Dehan's speech. Now she started saying, "No, no, no! *No!* You can't do this! It was my mother! You *know* it was my mother! I *left*! I dropped her at Mrs. Rodriguez's and I *left*!"

Dehan sighed and shook her head. "Come on, Theresa, you can't honestly expect us to believe that."

Suddenly Theresa's face flushed with color and she leaned forward, pounding her small fist on the table.

"What? You can't find my mother, so you decide to go for me? Because I had a lesbian affair?" Her voice became shrill. "All this time it has been my damned mother! Now you hotshots come along and when it looks like your unbroken record is about to break, you shift to me because you think you can pin it on me. What jury doesn't like to hang a lesbian, right?"

Dehan's brow furrowed slightly. "So where *is* your mother?"

"*I don't know! And doesn't that tell you something?*" There was a moment of deafening silence. Then she said more quietly, "She is probably in California with that son of a bitch she was always talking about. Why don't you talk to him instead of hounding me?"

I spoke for the first time in a while. "We have him downstairs in a holding cell."

You don't often see people truly gape. Theresa gaped. Her jaw hung open, and her eyes went circular.

"You *found* him?"

I nodded. "But not in San Diego."

"Where?"

I smiled on my right side, where it looks most ironic. "Where is your mother, Theresa?"

"Again? I'm telling you I don't know. I-don't-*know*! *Ask him!*"

"Last time he heard from her was last Christmas."

She shook her head. "You're lying. *He's* lying! That's not possible. She killed Lilith, she took the car, and she went to him. It's a testament to the incompetence of the NYPD that you haven't found her. She's probably lying on a damned beach, sunning herself . . ."

"On what, Theresa?"

She looked bewildered. "On what? On a beach . . ."

I leaned forward and spoke loudly. "On *what*? She didn't run away with the family silver! She didn't clean out her account. She didn't cash in an insurance. She hasn't touched her credit card. So what the hell has she been living on for the last year?" She blinked three times but said nothing. I went on. "Are you feeding her? Have you got a cabin in the Adirondacks? Or the Ozarks or the Rockies in Colorado? You figure you'll have her declared dead in a year or two and claim the insurance? Where is she, Theresa?"

She clenched her fists and clutched them against her chest. Tears sprang into her eyes, and her face flushed red. "*I don't know! Maybe she is dead! I don't know!*"

Dehan stood and sighed loudly. "So now she's dead? Where's the body? It's not easy to lose a body, you know? Sooner or later it surfaces. And where's the car? Somebody is hiding your mother, Theresa, and we can prove that it is *not* Bobby Hansen!"

Dehan walked behind Theresa. I laid both my hands on the table, close to hers, and stared into her eyes.

"Something happened that night, Theresa, and you need to tell us what it was. You fought with Lilith, she threatened to tell Bill about you and her, you brought her home, she climbed out of the car and you watched her walk away . . ."

Dehan said, "What happened next?"

She leaned forward, her elbows pushing into her belly, her face buried in her hands. "I turned the car around and I drove home. Nothing else happened until Dad called me. I would never, never, *never* hurt Lilith! I *loved her*!"

Dehan snapped, "Now you loved her? You just got through saying . . ."

"*I was not in love with her! I loved her!*"

Dehan glanced at me. Theresa leaned forward and pointed at me. "You are trying to pin this murder on me because you can't find my mother. But even if you prosecute me for Lilith's death, you will still have to explain what happened to Mom. And any defense attorney worth his salt will tear your case apart!"

Dehan drew breath to speak, but I got in first.

"Can you afford a defense attorney worth his salt?"

Theresa stared at me as though I had slapped her in the face. I saw Dehan do a double take just behind her. I repeated, "Can you?"

"Yes," she said, "as a matter of fact I can."

I went on, "I couldn't help noticing, you have a private practice, for which you don't charge. Most junior doctors, struggling to get a place in a hospital, can't afford to do that kind of thing."

"So I have private means. What's that to you?"

"Mind telling me the source of those private means?"

"Yes, I do. Mind your own goddamn business!"

"Your dad helps you? There is no shame in that."

Her eyes were darting all over my face. The fear was there again. Finally she said, "Yeah, my dad helps me. So what?"

I shrugged. "So nothing."

"Are you planning to arrest me?"

I shook my head. "No, not yet, Theresa. You're free to go. But before you do, you ought to be aware that you are now our prime suspect in Lilith's death. If you know something, if you know where your mother is, if you have any information about what happened that night which you are withholding, now is the time to come forward."

She sagged back in her chair. "I have told you everything I know. Whatever happened, happened after I had left."

"You have no alibi, Theresa, you are aware of that."

"Yes, I realize that. But I did not kill her. I *loved* her! Why would I kill her?" We sat staring at each other in silence for a moment. Then she said suddenly, "Mom was left alone. Dad took Ern home. Mom was alone as Lilith walked past. She must have seen her. She was crazy. Rage could build in her in a matter of seconds. She saw Lilith, grabbed the scissors, and rushed out after her. When the rage had passed, she climbed in the car and just drove . . ."

Dehan spoke from the wall where she was leaning. "Straight into a fold in the space-time continuum, never to be seen again."

"I can't explain that, but . . ."

Dehan pushed off the wall and stepped forward. "I'll tell you what I think happened." She walked 'round the table and sat down. "I think you got out of the car and followed Lilith, aiming to have a last try at convincing her not to talk to Bill. But before you could catch up with her your mother appeared, running down the steps, and went after her. She killed her right there before your eyes. You reacted, in a panic, and told your mother to get the hell out of there. Maybe you sent her to the Bluebird, told her to pay cash. And next morning you went and collected her, disposed of the car somewhere, maybe in a lockup, and you've been hiding her ever since."

There was no emotion in Theresa's face as she listened to this. When Dehan had finished, she blinked once, slowly, and said, "You're out of your mind."

"Convince me why."

"Because I hate my mother, Detective, and if I had witnessed the scene as you describe it, I would have killed her myself, with my own bare hands."

TWELVE

I SAT WITH MY ASS ON MY DESK AND MY ARMS FOLDED
and examined the limp decorations that hung around the detectives' room, like your neighbor's underwear on the clothesline
after a rainstorm. Only shiny.

Dehan stood staring out of the window at the heavy clouds
that were moving in from the Atlantic again. I couldn't see her,
but I could sense her going up on her toes and coming down
again, with her hands in her pockets.

"Can I open the envelope?"

"No. And you mean 'may.' May I open the envelope."

"May I open the envelope?"

"It's still no."

"Because you're afraid you're wrong."

"No. I am certain I'm right."

She turned and came and stood next to me. Her face was
serious.

"What if she is dead, Stone?"

I studied her face a moment, thinking. "Okay, then we have
two big questions to answer. And they are harder than 'where is
she?' One, for what purpose was she killed? And two, the big one,
where the hell is her body? You said it yourself, a body is very hard

to dispose of. Especially a large body like hers. And remember, there was no trace in the house of any kind of violence."

"He took Ern home, and when he came back . . ." Her eyes were abstracted, with the cold light of the window on her face. She blinked and looked at me. "Tell me what you think happened, Stone. Stop playing games."

"It's pointless, I need proof."

"C'mon, don't be an asshole. If you have a viable theory . . ." She broke off because her phone had started ringing. She pulled it from her pocket and put it to her ear. "Dehan . . ."

She held my eye, chewing her lip as she listened. "Okay, we'll be there in half an hour." She hung up. "Ern has gone missing. They want us to look at the security footage."

I felt an empty pit in my stomach, grabbed my coat, and ran. I drove too fast for the freezing conditions, heading north along the Bronx River Parkway, snaking between cars, doing a hundred and ten where I should have been doing fifty. Dehan didn't speak. I figured she was making her peace with her gods.

We finally came off at Dobbs Ferry and broke the speed limit for two miles down Ashford Avenue and Broadway, till I skidded to a halt outside the clinic, and Dehan and I ran up the steps, taking them two at a time.

Dr. Fraser was waiting for us at the door again, but this time he did not look so complacent. As we entered the reception, he gripped my arm and led me across the oak-paneled lobby toward his office.

"Thank God you're here. I am worried, Detective Stone. I am very worried."

He opened the door and let us through. Dehan was asking, "Has he ever done anything like this before?"

"No! Not at all, and it makes no sense . . . Please, sit, sit!"

He gestured us to two chairs at his desk where there was a laptop set to face us. "Let me put you in the picture. I had my passive-aggressive group. It's a two-hour session, and my staff are instructed not to interrupt me unless it is a real emergency." He sighed and rubbed his face with his hands. "While I was engaged with that group, a woman turned up claiming to be Ernest's sister, Pat . . ."

Dehan cut him short. "You have her on camera?"

"Wait, yes, but I am coming to that. You need to hear this first. She showed her ID, which the girl on the desk thought was adequate. You must remember, this is *not* a prison. We do not have high-risk inmates here. Most of our clients are here for *their* protection, not society's.

"Fifteen minutes later, Mrs. Perkins and Ernest strolled out. The receptionist assumed that Ernest was saying goodbye to his sister. When she heard the car revving, she looked out and saw a dark blue BMW accelerating away down the drive. She saw no sign of Ernest. The gate is automatic for cars leaving the compound, and frankly we would have no reason, on the face of it, to stop Ernest from leaving with his sister. However, when my staff informed me, in view of your recent visit, I immediately reviewed the footage, and, well, see for yourselves . . ."

He pressed play on the laptop, and the screen was taken up with good-quality black-and-white footage of a dark BMW approaching along the drive. The plates were visible, and Dehan made a note, then stood and walked away to put out a BOLO.

Next it cut to the lobby and a very attractive, slim woman, probably in her mid to late forties, dressed in clothes that were not so much elegant as expensive, and revealing of a generously endowed figure. A hat did a lot to hide her face. She approached the desk, spoke to the receptionist, and signed a book. I pressed pause.

"I need that signature."

He pushed a piece of paper across the desk. "I have photo-copied it."

I took the photocopy. "I'm going to need the book. Don't let anybody else touch it. Have it put in a refuse sack. And the pen. Now!"

He got on the phone, and I pressed Play.

She left the lobby, and after that there were snatches of her in the ballroom where we had spoken to Ern, the two of them walking in the gardens, and then making their way through the lobby again and finally climbing in the car.

There was a tap at the door, and the pretty receptionist on the security footage brought in a refuse sack and placed it beside me. She started to apologize, but I cut her short.

"That's okay, there was no way you could have known. But I need you to think hard. Did she say anything to you, anything at all about where she might be going?"

She shook her head. "Just that she was Patricia Perkins, Ernest's sister, she had come to see him."

"No explanation as to why she had never come before?"

"No . . . wait! She did say she had been in California for the last year. She joked that she had been in a very different kind of clinic, and said that she had lost, I think she said, a hundred and twenty pounds. Then she said she couldn't wait to get back to Cali."

I turned to Fraser. "Okay, she has an hour's lead on us. You have an IT guy here?"

"Of course."

"Have him send this footage to the lab . . ." I scrawled Joe's email address on a piece of paper. "I'll call and tell him to expect it. Tell him to write 'Ref: Stone Perkins Footage' in the subject. I'll take the original, the visitors' book, and the pen."

Fraser got on the internal phone. I stood and called Joe.

"Stone, what's up?"

"I'm sending you some security footage. I need it an hour ago. I need the faces of the woman and the man leaving with her cleaned up and enlarged for a BOLO. The guy has been kidnapped from a clinic and his life is at risk."

I saw Dehan and Fraser turn and stare at me, but I ignored them and went on.

"There is a BOLO out on the car. I need a BOLO out on those two people now, Joe."

"I'm on it."

I hung up. Dehan was on her cell, reciting the license plate. ". . . and fast-track it. Lives are at risk."

We stepped back out into the cold. Dehan hadn't had time to put on her layers, and she was stamping and shivering, billowing condensation. Overhead the sky was blue, but in the east big clouds in various hues of gray were piling on top of each other.

I dumped the sack in the trunk, yanked open the door, and climbed in behind the wheel. Dehan slammed the door and said, "Put the heater on before I freeze."

I turned the key, and the engine roared as she turned up the heater.

"Dehan, only two people knew where Ern was. Pat didn't know. Cyril put him here after she'd left."

"I know. I was thinking that. But I don't know what it means. Did this happen because you told Theresa to contact her mother?"

Before I could answer, her cell rang. She fumbled it from her pocket. "Yeah, Dehan . . . Okay, thanks."

"It was a hire car. Hired this morning from Budget on East Forty-Third, three blocks from Grand Central."

"In what name?"

"Mrs. Patricia Perkins."

I called the chief at the 43rd. It rang twice, and he answered. "John . . ."

"Sir, Patricia Perkins hired a blue BMW this morning from Budget Car Rental. She hired it in her own name, and she must have used a credit card. We need those documents from Budget, we need to see if it's the same card she had before, and if it's not, we need a court order to view the new credit account."

"I'll see to it. You have a BOLO out?"

"Yes, sir. We're on our way to the lab now. She handled a visitors' book and a pen. She has an hour on us or a little more."

I hung up and pulled onto the driveway toward the gate. Dehan was silent till we were out on the road. Then she asked,

"Why do you think his life is at risk? What could he tell us that he hasn't already told us?" I didn't answer, and she narrowed her eyes and shook her head. "How could she even know that we had spoken to him, or restarted the investigation?"

I nodded. "She couldn't."

"Which means she *is* still in touch with somebody . . ."

"If that were true, it would have to be one of two people."

"Theresa or Cyril."

I nodded, accelerating fast down Ashford toward the I-87.

"That doesn't make a lot of sense."

"Not much in this case does."

"Whoever it is paid for her to stay in that private clinic. At least that explains why we couldn't find her, she was re-creating herself . . ."

"But that raises two big questions, Dehan. The first is how the hell she paid for it . . ."

She frowned at me. "Yeah, there is a hell of a lot of money being thrown around here, by people who shouldn't be able to afford it."

I nodded again and went on, "And the other is, if she was in the process of changing her identity, why the hell did she suddenly leave the private clinic and show up here to snatch Ern, using her old ID and credit card? She must have known she'd be spotted."

"That doesn't make any sense at all."

I sighed. "It only makes sense if . . ."

"If she doesn't know she is wanted for murder." I stared at her for a moment. "Eyes on the road! It's been snowing, remember? Stone, it makes sense if she does not know that she is wanted for murder."

"You said that. Care to explain how her scissors got into Lilith's back, with her prints all over them, and she fled the scene in her car and disappeared for a year without realizing she was wanted for murder?"

She raised both hands palm down and made a slow patting motion. "Slow down, Sensei. Hear me out. Now, baby steps, listen to me. Let's imagine for a moment that Pat did not kill Lilith."

"Who did?"

"Shut up. Let's imagine that Theresa killed Lilith, but it was not a spontaneous, opportunistic murder. It was premeditated and carefully planned."

I frowned at the I-87 as I floored the pedal, and the big cat began to chew up the blacktop with a savage snarl.

I said, "Interesting. Explain that to me."

"Okay." She held up her hands like she was framing a picture. "Theresa has her moment of indiscretion. She has what she thinks is going to be a brief, passionate affair with Lilith. What she doesn't realize is that Lilith is infatuated with her and, once the affair gets under way, she falls in love. Now Theresa doesn't know how to get out of their romance, which is becoming more complicated and more dangerous every weekend."

"Dangerous . . . ?"

"Dangerous to Theresa in that it is a threat to her upcoming marriage and her future family and possibly her career."

"Agreed so far."

"So it goes down pretty much like Theresa said, except that Theresa decides two or three weeks beforehand what she is going to do . . ."

"Okay . . ."

"She steals the scissors from her mother, taking care to use surgical gloves, to which she has unlimited access. She stores the scissors in her car, and she arranges with Lilith and Mrs. Rodriguez, well in advance, what they are going to do that evening. And now comes the smart bit."

"She persuades her father . . ."

"Shut up. She persuades her dad that Ern has to go into a clinic."

"What does she achieve by doing that?"

"Lilith is a magnet for Ern. Wherever she goes he follows like a puppy dog. So she needs him out of the way on that day. And she needs her dad out of the way too. So she arranges with the clinic for him to move in on that day . . ."

"That is pure speculation . . ."

But even as I was saying it, she was pulling out her phone and calling the clinic.

"Dr. Fraser. Just confirm something for me, would you . . . The date of Ernest's admission . . ."

She put it on speaker.

". . . remember it well because it was so unusual. But it seemed there was a special family celebration, and so Ern would spend the morning at home and then be brought in after the Christmas luncheon."

"And who arranged that?"

"Well, I spoke to Mr. Perkins, but my understanding was that it was a family decision, so to speak."

"Thank you." She hung up. "With Ern and Cyril out of the way, she kills Lilith and plants the evidence to make it look like her mother did it."

"What for? And how can she guarantee that her mother is going to disappear?"

"What for? Because she hates her mother. How, the same way she got rid of Ern, by booking her into a private clinic where nobody would dream of looking for her."

"You know how much they charge for those places? Thousands, tens of thousands. How could she possibly afford it? And, more to the point, how could she persuade her to go, on Christmas Day? And it completely ignores the row that morning with Lilith and Gwen."

She shook her head. "Not necessarily, Stone. Again, baby steps, and remember, Theresa is very smart. She knows from past experience that as soon as Ern gets there, he is going to find the first opportunity to go over to Gwen's house, and Dad is going to follow because he is sweet on Gwen, and Gwen likes him."

I grunted. "Maybe."

"No maybe about it, Stone. She knows that, and she's right.

She also knows her mother pretty well, and it's a cinch for her to start winding her mom up days in advance about Lilith and Gwen and how they are homing in on Ern and especially Cyril. What are they after? Are they after the house? His money? They want to move in and kick her out?"

"This is speculation, Dehan."

"Yeah, but it also follows that she could use the same arguments to get her to sign on for the clinic, and have a limo pick her up while Cyril and Ern are out of the house. Remember, this woman, Pat, has a low IQ, and it is not hard to imagine Theresa convincing her. Hell, she could argue she's pulled strings among her medical colleagues, and Pat would buy right into it. Especially if she told her she was going to a swanky clinic full of the rich and the famous.

"If Dad knows nothing about it, to him it's going to look exactly as he described it. And Mom, who's as thick as two short planks, is going to buy the whole anonymity thing, forbidden to contact home, must lose a hundred and twenty pounds in a year and for that you have to be completely isolated. And above all, convince her she is going to win Cyril back, *and* have Hansen eating out of her hand."

I sighed. "It's far-fetched, Dehan."

"But it explains everything."

"Everything except one thing, one very important detail."

"What?"

"How the hell she could afford it."

She nodded. "I thought about that. You noticed that Theresa seems to have a lot of money for a struggling young doctor, remember?"

"Sure."

"So we need to look and see if Lilith had any insurance policies taken out on her life."

I blinked a few times at the shiny blacktop racing at me, with the vast, dark clouds piling up at the end of it. After a moment I said, "Huh."

"That's it? Huh?"

I shook my head. "No, it's a good theory, Dehan. Far-fetched, but good. It could be that way, only . . . We need to look at the insurance angle, and you need to explain to me why Pat has made a sudden reappearance now, just as we have started to look into the case again."

She sighed. "Yeah, that one has me a bit foxed. Why turn up now, and why take her brother out of the clinic?"

My phone pinged, and I pulled it from my jacket to look at the screen. There was an email there. I thumbed it open and glanced at the contents. I heaved a big sigh and slipped the phone back in my inside pocket. Dehan said, "What?"

I didn't answer for a long while. Finally, as we were approaching the Bruckner Expressway, I said, "You remember Gwen said Pat had some horrible ratlike dogs?"

She thought a moment. "Yeah, I remember. Why?"

"Has anybody else mentioned those dogs?"

She was quiet for a while. "No. Nobody. Why?"

I shrugged. "I'm just wondering what happened to the dogs."

THIRTEEN

We dropped the visitors' book and the pen with Joe and told him it was top priority, as lives were at stake. He said he'd put a rush on it and told us he'd sent the images from the security footage out to all the local precincts. If she was still in New York State, it would not be long before she, Ern, or the BMW was spotted.

We thanked him and headed out to the Albert Einstein College parking lot. There I stopped and drummed my fists gently on the roof of the car. Dehan stopped with her hand on the passenger door handle.

"You gonna let me in sometime soon, Stone?"

I stared at her a moment, noticed she didn't have her woolen hat on. Her cheeks were flushed red, and there were specks of sleet on her hair.

"Yeah, of course. Cyril or Theresa. We need to pull one of them in. Or both."

"Both."

"But we need . . ." I trailed away. "If your theory is right, we need to check the insurance papers . . ."

"We can be doing that while we grill them, Stone. That's a

couple of phone calls. What we need to grill them on is *how* Pat knew where Ern was, if the only people who knew were Theresa and Cyril."

"Yeah," I said, and unlocked the door. "And where are the damned dogs."

She pulled her door open, looking at me across the roof like I was mildly insane. "What is your obsession with those dogs, Stone? Maybe she took them to the clinic with her."

I tossed her the keys. "You drive. I need to make some calls." I dialed as we swapped sides of the car. The phone rang a couple of times, and a sweet voice answered.

"Vazquez. Drop what you're doing." I climbed in the car and slammed the door as Dehan gunned the engine. "I want you to call all the vets around Pugsley Park. Find out if Cyril or Theresa Perkins have taken any dogs in during the last year. Thanks."

I hung up. Dehan said, "Station house, coffee, call in Patricia and Cyril, interrogate them both. One of them was in touch with Pat."

"Okay, agreed, meantime we get Chavez to look up the insurance. What are we looking for?" I frowned. "To see if Theresa Perkins had taken out any insurance on Lilith Jones?"

"Yeah, I can't see how else she could afford her mother's clinic."

I scratched my head. "But she would have had to pay something up front. Where did she get that from? And, while we're at it, how can her dad afford that surgery on Lenox?"

She didn't get a chance to answer because my cell rang again. It was Dispatch. I put it on speaker.

"Detective Stone, the blue BMW you had a BOLO on has been spotted. It is parked in the lot at the Bluebird Motel, on Long Beach . . ."

I snapped, "I know where it is. We're on our way."

The Jag bucked as Dehan floored the pedal. Dispatch was saying, "The patrol are requesting instructions as to what to do. I'm patching you through, Detective."

"Patrolman Horowitz, Detective. What do you want us to do?"

"Watch the car. Don't let it leave. There is only one exit to that parking lot. Block it discreetly. We're on our way. Inquire from the receptionist what room they're in. Keep a low profile."

"You got it, Detective."

Fifteen minutes later, we pulled up outside the Bluebird Motel. The NYPD patrol car was parked beside the sidewalk but blocking the exit from the parking lot at the back of the hotel. We climbed out and approached the two patrolmen. I showed them my badge. "Detective Stone, this is Detective Dehan, Forty-Third Precinct. Where's the car?"

"Patrolman Horowitz, this is Bernstein." He pointed toward the back of the building. "The BMW is still parked in back, outside room 302. The manager says it was a woman in fancy clothes, might have been a high-class hooker, and a guy who looked . . ." He hesitated. "Like, mentally challenged."

"Who'd they sign in as?"

"Mr. and Mrs. Smith."

"Original."

"What do you want to do, sir?"

"Take the car in. Park behind the BMW so it can't pull out. Be ready to provide backup if required."

"Ten four, Detective."

We got back in the cars, and I pulled into the lot with the patrol car behind me. I parked beside the BMW, and Horowitz pulled up just behind it so it was boxed in. Then Dehan and I climbed out and we approached the door. I rapped on the wood and pressed the bell. Dehan shouted, "NYPD! Detectives Dehan and Stone. Patricia Perkins, if you're in there, open the door!"

There was only silence. I turned to Horowitz. "Go get the manager. Tell him to bring a key."

He ran across the lot, puffing condensation like a small, dark blue dragon. I hammered on the door again and rang the bell.

"Open up! NYPD. Patricia Perkins, this is Detective Stone of the New York Police Department. There is a warrant out for your arrest. If you do not open up, I am authorized to force the door! Open up!"

Again there was only silence. I watched Horowitz and the manager hurrying back across the lot. Horowitz approached at a jog and handed me the key. I gestured everybody to the side of the door, crouched down, and slipped the key in the lock. Nothing happened. The patrolmen and Dehan already had their weapons in their hands. I pulled my Sig Sauer, turned the key with my left hand, and pushed gently. The door swung inward with a small creak.

Nothing happened again. I peered in. It was dark, and all I could see were shadows. I stood, holding my weapon out in front of me, and shouted, "NYPD! Show yourselves!"

Dehan came in behind me and snapped on the light. Ern was there, on the bed. There was an almost empty box of donuts on the bedside table beside him. His eyes were dull and dilated. There was no sign that he had thrashed or convulsed. His skin was an unpleasant blue color. In his left hand were a few strands of dark hair. There was no sign of Pat.

I moved to the bathroom door and pushed it open. It was empty. Dehan was on her phone calling it in. I went to the manager, who was standing framed in the doorway, his jaw sagging and his eyes bulging. He said, "What happened?"

"You got CCTV?"

"Course."

"Let's go take a look-see." I turned to Horowitz. "Seal the area, including the BMW, don't let anybody in or out. Wait here for the crime scene officers."

"Ten four, Detective."

Dehan fell in beside me as we followed the manager back across the lot to the front of the hotel. She stared up at me as we walked, her eyes narrowed. "Have you *any* idea what's going on? Why? *Why* would she do this?"

"She didn't."

"What?"

I didn't answer. We followed the manager up the stairs to his small, cramped melamine office, where he showed us the CCTV footage for the last hour. We saw the BMW pull up outside the room. He said, "Booked her into the room at this stage. Paid cash. Very attractive woman. Stylish."

We watched them climb out of the car and go into the room. She was holding several items, amongst which I recognized the box of donuts. Nothing happened, and I fast-forwarded. At just short of fifteen minutes, she came out and slammed the door. She hesitated outside the car and then crossed the lot at a tottering run, out of sight.

I pulled out my cell and called Joe.

"Stone, I was about to call you. I'm on my way to Long Beach. I got a hit on the prints."

"It's not Pat Perkins, is it?"

"No."

"Hang on." I put it on speaker. "Okay, go ahead."

"Her name is Mary O'Connor, otherwise known as Zeta Finesse, a high-class escort for the less discerning gentleman on an expense account. She's been pulled in a few times, but her boyfriends' lawyers have got her off on technicalities."

Dehan made a face like a brain-ache. "Mary O'Connor? *Zeta Finesse?* Are you kidding me? What the hell, Stone?"

I couldn't help laughing. "Okay, Joe, thanks. When you get here, the victim has a few strands of dark hair in his left hand. I need you to rush me a DNA test on them. I need to know if the hair also belongs to Mary O'Connor. This case has more twists than a 1950s beach party."

"I have rapid DNA testing equipment in the van, John. I can run a sample of the hair, but it will only be informative. You can't use the result at trial. We're not allowed to use it on crime scene samples, only on individuals. I'll have to repeat the test back at the lab, and that will take longer."

I thought about it. "Yeah, okay. Off the record. I need to know, and I need to know fast, Joe."

I hung up. Dehan was still staring at me. "Why the hell wouldn't it be Mary O'Connor's hair, Stone? And while you're at it, why the hell has a high-class hooker killed Ern? Did I step through the looking glass somewhere along the line?"

I shook my head. "It's not as complicated as it looks, Dehan . . ."

"Oh, and while we're at it, more twists than a 1950s beach party? Seriously, Stone?"

I shrugged. "It just kind of popped out. Spontaneous."

"Spontaneous. You need a holiday."

"I'm getting one. A week in Hawaii. We made some assumptions at the start of the case, Dehan. You need to go back and un-assume them. Then everything will start to make sense."

"Even Mary O'Connor, the high-class hooker?"

"Even she."

We stepped out onto the porch. An icy wind poked steel-cold fingers through our clothes and made our skin crawl. Dehan hugged herself as she picked her way down the steps to the sidewalk. In the distance we could hear the wail of sirens.

"Stone, tell me something," she said through chattering teeth. "Was *any* of my theory in the car correct?"

I nodded. "Oh yes, a lot of it."

"Oh," she said, and gave a small laugh. "Cool."

We crossed the parking lot, back toward the room and Ern's lifeless body. At the door I paused and examined the lock. Dehan pulled her cell from her pocket, thumbed it a few times, and handed it to me.

"Here you go, Sherlock."

I took it and looked at it. "You have an app for a magnifying glass?"

"It's the camera, Stone, on zoom."

I sighed softly and examined the lock again while Dehan watched me.

"You think there was a third person in the room?"

"Well, there's no sign the lock has been picked." I handed her back her phone. "But I am wondering why a high-class escort, albeit one for undiscerning gentlemen, would want to poison Ernest Hartwell. Posing as his sister is strange enough; killing him is just too improbable to be credible."

"So she was employed to collect him and bring him here?"

"Hard to think of another reason."

I stepped inside and went around the bed to the bedside table. I stood a moment looking down at Ern. He looked oddly peaceful.

"Like he died in his sleep," I said, and glanced at Dehan, who was also staring down at him. "Only with his eyes open."

She nodded. "No convulsions, no violence, apparently no pain. What does that?"

"'My heart aches,'" I quoted, "'and a drowsy numbness pains my sense, as though of hemlock I had drunk . . .'" She raised an eyebrow at me. I said, "John Keats, 'Ode to a Nightingale.'"

I pulled on a pair of latex gloves from my pocket and picked up one of the donuts. I squeezed it. It was hard.

"Hemlock kicks in after about half an hour, but it takes several hours to kill. I'm figuring it was in the donuts. They are stale, probably bought yesterday and laced with an infusion from the leaves, and he's likely been eating them all morning. He's probably had enough to kill a horse, and when he started getting ill, Miss Finesse probably ran."

"So our killer was not necessarily here . . ."

Outside the air was full of sirens and the sound of vehicles pulling up outside the room. I pointed to the strands of hair in Ern's fingers. "I'm just wondering who that hair belongs to."

She bent closer and stared at it. "I guess Joe's about to tell us. What makes you think it's not Mary O'Connor's?"

I shrugged. "No convulsions, no struggle . . ."

We stepped outside again into the failing, frosted light under heavy clouds. Joe was there with his team, at the back of his van, climbing into his spaceman suit. He smiled as we approached.

"Crazy case, huh?"

"*Coitus mentalis.*" He laughed. I went on, "I think you're going to find the donuts laced with hemlock."

"Oh, interesting choice."

"Yeah, a compliant victim described by somebody as mentally retarded and subnormal. The effects would not be obvious to Zeta Finesse until they were well advanced." He made a face and nodded. "But what I need, as soon as you can possibly get it, is the identity of the hair. You're going to find it in the system, Joe. I'm sure of that."

"Tell me who you think it is. I'll check it for a match. Quicker than a full search."

I hesitated a moment and glanced at Dehan, then back at Joe. "I think it belongs to Pat Perkins."

Dehan shook her head. "*What?*"

Joe frowned. "*Coitus sanctus.* Seriously?"

"Maybe. It would be helpful to know. I'll be at the Perkinses' house. Let me know as soon as you get a result, will you?"

"Sure. I'll call you."

We climbed in the car, and I pulled out of the lot onto Broadway. Dehan raised both hands and shook her head. "You need to drive very slowly, and probably stop somewhere for a coffee and a large slice of pie. I am lost and *very* confused." She turned her hands palm up and shrugged. "What . . . *why?* I mean . . . *what?*"

I gave an indulgent laugh which I knew was annoying and, for good measure, added, "Those are very open questions, Dehan."

"Don't give me that crap, Stone. You are telling me you think Patricia Perkins got out of her clinic in California, came all the way to New York, and employed Mary O'Connor, aka Zeta Finesse, to abduct her brother from *his* clinic, feed him poisoned donuts, and bring him to this *particular* hotel so she could watch him die while he stroked her hair?"

"Well, sure," I said, suppressing a laugh, "when you say it like *that* it sounds improbable."

She made a smile that was more like a poke in the eye with a sharp stick. "Say it some way where it doesn't sound improbable."

I shook my head. "I'm not sure yet. But I repeat, Dehan, you are hanging on to suppositions we made at the start, which are not actually supported by facts."

"What supposition?"

"You know my methods, Watson, apply them! Besides, if I told you, then you wouldn't have to take me to Hawaii."

She grunted. "Okay, the first assumption was that Patricia Perkins had murdered Lilith through some kind of twisted jealousy."

"Correct."

"But now, increasingly, the evidence seems to point to her daughter, Theresa." She held up the fingers of her right hand. "The fact that Patricia was sent to, and admitted to, an expensive private clinic speaks to the pulling of strings among colleagues. The use of poison, the fact that she was the last person to see Lilith alive, *and* the fact that she had motive and opportunity all point to Theresa rather than her mother. So I have abandoned that assumption, Stone. I still don't see the purpose for this elaborate ruse."

I pulled over outside the Gentle Brew coffee shop and killed the engine.

"Let me ask you, Dehan, what would a person gain by getting Mary O'Connor to impersonate Pat Perkins?"

She thought for a long time, frowning. "Well, for a start, because Mary O'Connor looks nothing like Pat, it would allow her to go to the clinic without attracting attention and without triggering any of the BOLOs on the way."

I nodded, and she went on. "It would also allow Pat to be somewhere else, like the hotel room, waiting . . ."

I nodded again. "And, had Mary had more brains, or been

better instructed, it would have refocused attention on Pat as a suspect, while at the same time explaining her disappearance."

She nodded several times. "Yeah, I see that." She frowned again. "But the hair . . . ?"

"Yup," I said, and opened the door to get out. "The hair is the clincher."

FOURTEEN

SHE DIDN'T SPEAK TO ME AGAIN UNTIL SHE HAD finished her coffee and her blueberry pie but occasionally frowned at me resentfully. I tried to make light conversation by commenting, "If we take our time over coffee, it will give Joe time to analyze the hair."

But that just made her frown harder and glare out the window at the heavy blue-gray clouds and the hunched people walking quickly with their hands in their padded jackets.

We pulled up outside Cyril Perkins' house on Pugsley Avenue about forty-five minutes later. We knocked and rang, but there was no reply. I tried his cell but with the same result. I looked up at the sky. A few specks of sleet were beginning to fall. I pulled out my cell and called Theresa.

"Yes?"

"Dr. Perkins, this is Detective Stone."

"Oh, I'm Dr. Perkins again, am I? That's nice of you. Does that mean you no longer suspect me of murder?"

"I have some news. I'm here at your father's house, but he's not in. Any idea where he is?"

"People have lives, Detective. Perhaps he's doing some Christmas shopping. Or maybe he's out murdering somebody."

"Yeah, perhaps. Ordinary people with ordinary lives do that too, Dr. Perkins. Are you at your surgery?"

"I will be in about an hour. Why?"

"I told you, I need to give you and your father some news."

There was a long silence. "About Mom?"

"Yes."

"Have you found her?"

"Maybe."

"What's that supposed to mean?"

"It's easier if we meet and talk, Dr. Perkins. We'll see you at the surgery in an hour."

"Fine."

"By the way, Doctor, your mother had some dogs, right?"

"Yes, a couple of terriers, why?"

"Did she take them with her?"

"No, why?"

"What happened to them?"

"Dad kept them for a while. Then they died. They were old. Why?"

There was a bleep. I looked at the screen and saw I had a call waiting from the station. "Listen, I have a call waiting. I'll see you at your surgery in an hour."

I hung up, then said, "Yeah, Maria, what is it?"

"The Jacobi called. They have a case of suspicious poisoning. The victim is critical and in the ICU."

"So . . . ?"

"I know you're only doin' cold cases, John, and I was gonna send somebody else. But then I seen the name of the victim. It's Mary O'Connor. They don't know if she's gonna make it."

"Jesus!" I glanced at Dehan. "Thanks, Maria. We'll get right over there." I hung up. "Mary O'Connor. She's at the Jacobi, poisoned. She's critical, might not make it."

"Holy . . . !"

"Tying up loose ends."

"Come on, we have to get there. You never know, she might recover consciousness."

But she didn't recover consciousness. She was dead by the time we got there. We were met outside the ICU by a Dr. Fenninger, a pale, blond woman with bleached blue eyes that looked like they'd been left too long in the sun. She looked tired.

"Detectives, there isn't much I can tell you at this stage. The ambulance service was notified by a cab driver. Apparently he'd picked her up in Long Beach and was headed for Manhattan. She began to display very odd behavior and he pulled over to see if she was okay. From what he said, she seemed to be paralyzed. By the time they got her here she was almost comatose. It was too late to do anything."

Dehan asked, "Any idea what caused it?"

Fenninger shook her head. "Too soon to say. They'll do a full tox screen at the autopsy. Then they'll be able to tell you more." She hesitated. "But there aren't many substances that will kill you that way."

I said, "Hemlock will."

She nodded. "That's the first thing that springs to mind, but it is very difficult to take it by accident."

"Where are her personal effects?"

"They've been taken down to the forensic lab for testing." She hesitated again. "Obviously Forensics will inform you officially, but she had two sets of ID. Her own driver's license, in the name of Mary O'Connor, and then another one in a different name."

"Okay, thank you, Dr. Fenninger. I appreciate your help."

She walked away, and Dehan turned to me. "She ate a donut?"

"Maybe, but I don't think so. I suspect when the footage from that security camera at the Bluebird is analyzed fully, it's going to show somebody entering that room a lot earlier, with a key, and leaving well after Mary O'Connor did. That person administered the poison to her. Probably in a drink."

"Who?"

"I can't prove it yet."

My cell rang.

"Yeah, Stone."

"Stone, it's Joe."

"Where are you?" I put it on speaker.

"I just got back to the lab. Sam and Polly are finishing up at the hotel. I have the results from the hair Ernest was holding in his fingers. You were right. It belongs to his sister, Patricia Perkins. How did you know?"

"Lucky guess. Mary O'Connor was brought into the Jacobi a while ago. It sounds as though she was poisoned with the same substance that killed Ernest. Her personal effects have just been sent down. Among them two driver's licenses, one in her name and another in somebody else's. Two gets you twenty it's Pat Perkins'. Joe, fingerprints on that other license are a priority. Have you got it there?"

There was some noise of bustling, and after a moment he said, "Yeah, here it is."

"Is it Pat Perkins'?"

A small laugh. "Yes, it is."

"I know what you're going to find. You're going to find only Pat's prints. That document has been stashed in an envelope in a drawer for the past year, but I need you to confirm that for me, Joe. Soon as you can, pal."

"Okay, I'll do it now and get back to you. Frank's got the body?"

"Yeah. It's just been sent down."

"Okay, I'll call you as soon as I've confirmed the license."

"Thanks, Joe."

I hung up. Dehan was walking away from me talking on the phone. I could hear her saying, ". . . This is a top priority, and she should be considered dangerous. She is wanted for three homicides. The photograph is a year old, and she may have lost a lot of weight since."

I said, "What was that?"

"BOLO for Pat. She can't have got very far. Stone, we should talk to the media, publish her photograph and have a computer simulation of what she would look like if she had lost weight. This woman is on a rampage and has to be stopped."

"I thought your money was on Theresa."

"But Pat was there, Stone! You heard what Joe said. That was Pat's hair in his fingers." She shook her head. "I'm sorry, Stone, but I think you're overcomplicating this. Pat killed Lilith out of jealousy and went on the run, with or without Theresa's help. Maybe Theresa helped her get into a clinic. I don't know, but now she's back, and she is killing off loose ends."

"How did Mary O'Connor get Pat's driver's license?"

"Pat gave it to her, so she could get Ern out of the clinic."

"What for?"

"Hell, Stone! Maybe she went crazy when she lost weight, I don't know! But that was her hair in Ern's hand. She was there!"

I nodded. "Okay, let's go find Perkins and give him and Theresa the news."

We rode the elevator down to the ground floor, and as we stepped out into the parking lot, I called Perkins again. This time he answered on the second ring. He sounded sleepy.

"Hello?"

"Mr. Perkins, this is Detective Stone. I've been trying to reach you."

"I'm sorry, I was asleep. I often have a nap during the early afternoon, after luncheon. A sign I am growing old, I suppose. How can I help you?"

"We have an update on the case, and I'd like to put you and Theresa up to speed."

"Oh, I see. Well, by all means. Is it something you can tell me over the telephone?"

"Not really. I would rather see you both in person, if that's okay."

"Surely. I don't know what my daughter's timetable is like . . ."

"She's free now, at her surgery. Can we meet there, Mr. Perkins?"

"In Harlem . . . ?"

"If that's inconvenient, we can pick you up."

"No, no, not at all. I'll be there."

He hung up, and I slipped the telephone into my pocket. Then I stopped dead in my tracks and stared straight ahead. The burgundy glint of my car seemed strangely intense in the dull gray shade of the naked trees. Dehan stopped and stared back at me. "What is it?"

"Her surgery," I said.

"What are you talking about, Stone?"

"Pat. She's at the surgery."

"Holy crap! You think she's going to try to kill Theresa?"

She didn't give me time to answer. She was off at a run, sprinting down the path toward the Jag. I went after her. She reached the driver's door before me and shouted, "Keys!"

I threw them to her and moved to the passenger door. She fired up the engine and was moving as I climbed in and slammed the door. We burned rubber out of the hospital compound as she asked me, "Is it a hunch, or do you know something?"

"No, I don't know for certain, Dehan. That wasn't what . . ." I sighed. "It's a hunch."

"Stone! We can't call for backup on a hunch! Is Theresa's life in imminent danger?"

I drew breath to answer, but she swore violently, grabbed the radio, and called Dispatch.

"This is Detective Carmen Dehan, I need a patrol car immediately at five thirty-one Malcolm X Boulevard, at the surgery of Dr. Theresa Perkins. Instruct officers to call me as soon as they arrive and to proceed with caution."

When she put down the radio, I said, "I don't think Theresa's life is in danger, Dehan."

"Call her."

I called. It rang and went to voicemail. I dialed again with the same result. I dialed a third time. I was beginning to worry, then her voice said, "Yes, Dr. Perkins here."

"Doctor, it's Detective Stone."

"Detective, this is becoming tedious."

"I agree. Your father is on his way. We'll arrive in about twenty minutes, traffic permitting. Before that a patrol car will turn up to make sure you're safe. Please just give them some coffee and ask them to wait for us to arrive."

"To make sure I'm okay? Why?"

"I'll explain when we get there."

I heard a noisy sigh, and she hung up without saying goodbye. I slipped the phone into my pocket, and we drove on in silence and at great speed into the growing gloom.We arrived at her surgery twenty-five minutes later. The patrol car was parked at the main entrance to the block, but aside from that there was no sign that anything was wrong. The patrolman had called to say all was well and to ask for instructions. Dehan had told him to wait there until we arrived.

When we pushed into her consulting room, we found her sitting behind her desk with the two cops drinking coffee and her father sitting on the couch. They all looked at us without much humor, and the patrolman, a six-foot-three black guy with a chest like a wooden beer cask, said, "You done wasting our time, Detectives?"

I smiled at him pleasantly. "Don't be hard on yourself, Officer. Two people were murdered today." I pointed at the window. "The presence of your patrol car out there might well have avoided it being three. Thank you for your help, we can take it from here."

He grunted, and he and his partner left with a "You have a nice day."

The door closed behind them, and Theresa and her father sat and stared at us. It was Theresa who spoke first.

"You said you had some news, Detective."

Dehan sat on the arm of the couch, and I pulled one of the chairs around from the desk and sat so I could see everyone.

"Your uncle"—I looked over at Cyril, who was frowning—"your brother-in-law, Ernest. He left his clinic this morning, early."

Cyril leaned forward. His face, half-amused, half-incredulous, said he thought I was insane. "He *left* the clinic? That's absurd, Detective. It is also impossible. They have strict instructions not to let him leave the premises unaccompanied."

I nodded and looked down at my shoes. Dehan said, "But he was accompanied."

Theresa stared at her father, who was staring at Dehan. Finally he said, "By whom? Who accompanied him?"

I stared at him until he looked at me, so I could read his face. I said, "A high-class escort known as Zeta Finesse . . ."

I couldn't finish because he exploded, his face crimson and his eyes bright. "*What? An escort? What in the name of . . . !*" He turned to Theresa. "Have you got Fraser's number? I swear to God I'll have his job!"

"Calm down, Mr. Perkins."

"*Calm down?*"

"Dr. Fraser had no idea she was an escort. More to the point, he did not know that Ernest would receive a visit today."

"I think you'd better explain yourself."

"Zeta, or, more precisely, Mary O'Connor, arrived unexpectedly, early in the morning, claiming to be Ernest's sister, Patricia Perkins." There was a deathly silence in the room. I went on, "Not only that, but she showed proof of ID, in the form of a driver's license."

Perkins sank back into the sofa. He had gone pale. "Sweet mother of God, what does it mean?"

"She explained to the receptionist that she had lost a lot of weight, over a hundred and twenty pounds, because she had been . . ." I turned and studied Theresa's face as I said it. "She had been at a private clinic in California for the last year."

Theresa had gone pale too. "A private clinic? That's why you couldn't trace her . . ."

I gave a small laugh. "But, Dr. Perkins, it was *not* your mother. It was an escort, with your mother's driver's license."

She shook her head. "I don't understand. How did this escort get hold of Mom's driver's license? And why, what purpose . . . ?"

"I'm coming to the purpose, Dr. Perkins. The question I have, the question that is really troubling me, is how did Mary O'Connor know that Ernest was at that particular clinic? Even if she was, as you seem to assume, Dr. Perkins, acting on the instructions of your mother, how could your mother possibly have known that Ernest was at Dr. Fraser's clinic? The only two people who knew where Ernest was were you and your father. So how did Mary O'Connor, or indeed Patricia Perkins, find out where he was? One of you needs to explain."

You could have heard a pin drop on the carpet. Theresa stared down at the edge of her desk and placed her fingertips on it. Cyril made rhomboid shapes with his fingers and thumbs and stared at them, like he was wondering if he'd got them right. Finally he said, "It was me, I told her."

FIFTEEN

I said, "You told Patricia Perkins that Ernest was at Dr. Fraser's clinic, the St. George?"

"Yes."

Theresa was watching her father with eyes that were almost bulging. Her voice was a rasp. "*Dad . . . !*"

Dehan shifted her position to squint at him. "So, all this time you have known where she was?"

He shook his head. "No, you don't understand. Theresa and I had discussed putting Ernest in a clinic for some time. He was miserable where he was living, out at Hunts Point. He was often teased and mocked in the street. It's a rough area, and frankly we were very concerned for his well-being. So we talked about it, but we were worried that Pat would not agree. She was . . ." He hesitated. "Well, not to put too fine a point on it, she is mean with money, unless she is spending it on herself. But once we had made all the arrangements, I told her. I said it was done, we were bound by contract with the clinic, that Theresa had made the necessary arrangements, and there was nothing she could do about it. That wasn't strictly true, but she believed it and accepted it. There is no doubt at all that Ernest is much happier at the clinic than he was in that awful place where he was shacked up."

Dehan asked, "When did you tell her?"

He shook his head and pushed out his bottom lip. "It must have been just a few days before Christmas, because he was due to move in on Christmas Day."

I frowned and scratched my chin. "I've been wanting to ask you about that. It's a very odd day to move in, don't you think?"

He shrugged. "Perhaps. We discussed it, and we thought it would be nice for him. All the celebrations and decorations would make him feel more welcome."

I looked over at Theresa, who was the color of bread dough. "You agreed with all this, Dr. Perkins?"

She nodded. "Yes."

"And it was your task, Mr. Perkins, to drive him up to the clinic after Christmas luncheon?"

"That's correct, as I have already explained to you."

"Meanwhile Pat was left alone at the house."

"Yes . . ."

"Because you, Dr. Perkins, were . . ." She swallowed, and I said, "Otherwise engaged." I stood and walked to the window, looking out at the lamplit people, bowing their way through the sleet and the gathering sludge.

"So the theory is that while you, Dr. Perkins, were otherwise engaged and Mr. Perkins was driving Ernest to the clinic, your mother saw Lilith returning home through the front window, she grabbed her scissors, and raced down and stabbed her in the back. Then, realizing what she had done, she jumped in her car and drove off to California where she had booked herself into a private clinic for a year, without telling anyone." I turned and looked at them both. "To say that that is improbable is the understatement of the century."

He was frowning, like I was talking to him in Greek. "I don't know what you're saying?"

I smiled and gave a small laugh. "Let me see if I can make this simple." I held up my index finger. "One, what was clear to me from day one, it was impossible for Pat to disappear so completely without a prearranged plan. Two, whether she went herself or arranged for Mary O'Connor to go on her behalf, there was no way for Pat to know that Ernest was at that clinic unless one of you told her." I gestured at Cyril. "And it turns out that it was you, Mr. Perkins, who told her. So was it you, also, who helped her plan her escape?"

He shook his head. "No, of course not. That makes no sense at all. Lilith's murder was not a planned act. How could anyone have known that Lilith was going to be there at that time on that day? Besides, I loved Lilith like family. Why would I conspire to have her killed and then send Pat away? That would be madness!"

I looked down at Theresa, sitting at her desk. The gloom was closing in, and the lamp on her desk made a warm amber pool around her hands.

"Is that right, Theresa? Could anybody have known that Lilith was going to be at that place at that time on that day? Could anybody have planned that? Could anybody have had a motive to kill Lilith?"

She shook her head, but she wouldn't look at me. "No."

Cyril was staring at us both by turns. "What is he saying, Theresa? What is he getting at? Theresa . . . ?"

"Nothing! It's bullshit! They are trying to suggest that I killed Lil!"

"*You?*" He stared at us like the world had gone mad. "Are you out of your minds? Why in God's name would Theresa murder Lilith? They were like sisters!"

Dehan said, "One of you helped to conceal Pat for the last year. Nobody else could have done it . . ."

Cyril held out his hand, palm up, like he was offering canapés. "What about this Robert, Bobby Hansen! She was forever talking about him and how she was going to go to him . . ."

Dehan cut him short. "He's in a holding cell right now at the Forty-Third. He was living in Philadelphia, on his own, in what looked like a squat. He last heard from Pat last Christmas. And for the record, Mr. Perkins, he was too stupid to hide the invisible man's shorts, let alone make Pat disappear. She did not go to Bobby Hansen, and even if she had, we would have found her. Pat went completely off the radar for a year. For that she needed help."

There was a deathly silence while Perkins stared at his daughter and she stared at her hands. I spoke into that silence.

"She vanished without a trace for a year. That is very hard to do. And now, suddenly, just as we start our investigation, she resurfaces. She employs an escort who looks nothing like her to impersonate her, and she gives her her driver's license to help her pull it off. And she does all of this with one purpose, and one purpose only."

Theresa raised her head at last and looked at me, knitting her brows. "What purpose?"

"To murder Ernest."

Cyril covered his face with his hands and started to sob. Theresa was shaking her head, and her face was crumpling. She kept whispering, "*No, no . . .*"

Cyril dragged his hands down from his face, and his cheeks were wet and shiny with tears. "How?" he asked.

"We'll have to wait for the autopsy report. But it looks like he was poisoned."

His face twisted with incomprehension. "*Poisoned?* How? What with? Surely poison is almost impossible to get hold of these days!"

Then he froze, glanced at his daughter a moment, and then stared at his feet. Theresa was rigid, looking hard at her desk with wide eyes. "I was at home with my husband and my baby, then I was at the hospital, and then I came straight here. I have *hundreds* of witnesses who saw me! *I did not kill Lilith, and I did not kill Uncle Ern! This is insane! Mom killed Lilith, and now she has killed her brother because she is a crazy fucking psycho!*"

The silence that followed had the quality of ringing steel. It was hard and cold. I looked down at Cyril on the couch.

"Is that what she is, Cyril? A crazy fucking psycho?"

He gave his head a small shake. "No."

"You said you loved her. That most people didn't appreciate how lovely she was. She was warm and funny and loving . . ."

Theresa was staring at me, expressionless. Then she turned and stared at her father.

"Dad?"

He shook his head again like he was shaking away a fly. "Don't, Theresa. You don't know her the way I do . . ."

"She's a psychotic bitch, Dad! And you know it! I have hated her since the day I was born, and so have you!"

"That's not the impression you gave us, Mr. Perkins. You gave us the impression that you loved her dearly."

"People say things . . . Home life is never easy. Especially with Pat, she was a handful." He appealed to his daughter. "She was a handful, wasn't she? But . . ."

Theresa shut him down. "A handful? *A fucking handful? If you call tearing my hair out by the roots when I was just five fucking years old a fucking handful, yes! It was a handful of my fucking hair! If you call slapping me across the face every time I looked at her sideways a handful, yes! If you call her hitting you in the face with a hot fucking frying pan a handful, yes, Dad! She was a fucking handful! Shall I go on?*"

He had his eyes closed, and he kept shaking his head and shaking his hands, trying to hush her. There was a steady, quiet stream of words issuing from his mouth. "No, honey, no, stop now, stop, stop, please . . ." and so it went on until Theresa ran out of steam.

I gave them a moment to assimilate what had just happened and then asked him, "Where is she, Mr. Perkins?"

"No, nowhere. She's nowhere. I don't know. I don't know where she is."

"Dad . . . ?"

I pressed him. "You really loved her, huh? In spite of everything she did to you and your daughter, in spite of the violence and the poisoned, toxic relationship, you loved her."

He nodded, without looking at me, spoke mechanically. "She was funny, warm."

"Dad, are you out of your *mind*?"

"You were married once before, weren't you, Mr. Perkins?"

He remained very still, and after a moment said, "Yes."

"What was she like?"

Now he looked up at me and held my eye. "Servile. It was a bad mistake. She was very submissive, like a slave. She did everything I told her and treated me as though I were her master. I found it very unsettling and very uncomfortable. Eventually we separated. She went back to the Philippines, and I filed for divorce."

"Yeah, see, I did some checking, and it turns out you took out life insurance on your wife shortly after you were married, for a whopping two million dollars, and three years after she left you, you filed for a certificate of presumption of death, and then claimed on that two-million-dollar insurance. Now that struck me as very odd. Because most insurance companies are going to investigate a claim of that size, especially where there is no body. So I checked with the Philippines police department, and her family, and they all confirmed that your wife had never returned. So that does two things, Mr. Perkins. It makes you a prime suspect in the possible murder of your first wife, and it also puts you in possession of two million dollars. So, where is your *first* wife, Mr. Perkins?"

He took a deep breath and shoved his hands between his knees.

"I know it looks bad, but actually I have done nothing illegal. It is true that things were awful between me and Maui. She brought out the worst in me, and I ended up feeling disgust and contempt for her. I had in fact taken out mutual life insurance, for both of us. I own this house, I inherited it from my parents, and I had a good job, so I had disposable income, and I was planning to have children. So I wanted them to be taken care of if anything happened to either of us.

"After about a year of marriage I began to suspect that Maui was seeing other men, looking in fact for a better, richer husband. I checked her computer and found that she had joined several dating sites and was looking for a husband on the West Coast. She was very attractive and had several men interested.

"One day she just left. I tried to trace her. I informed the police. You didn't seem very interested, so I did my due diligence, and after three years I applied for a death certificate. I may have embellished a bit and said that she went trekking in the Colorado Mountains, but for all I know she did. She always said she wanted to. I got her death certificate and collected the insurance. It has helped me to take care of Theresa. To avoid exactly the sort of assumption you have made, I told people she had returned to the Philippines."

Dehan had been watching him with narrowed eyes. "That is one hell of a coincidence, Mr. Perkins. Two wives that go missing without a trace?"

He shook his head. "No, you don't understand. I detested Maui, but Pat was everything that Maui was not. She was strong and warm and full of life . . ."

"*Dad! Stop talking crazy, for Christ's sake!*"

He turned dull eyes on her. "Theresa, will you *please* just shut up!"

Another long, cold silence. Then Theresa said, "Dad . . . ? Where is she?"

"She *was* in a clinic, in California."

Dehan exploded, "And you have allowed the NYPD to waste valuable resources on a year-long wild goose chase, looking for a murder suspect that you were hiding?"

"I couldn't tell you where she was!"

"*Why?*"

"Because she needed help, and if I told you where she was, you would go storming in, arrest her and try her, and frame her for a murder she had not committed!"

I held up one hand. "Wait a minute. Wait a minute. How do you know she didn't kill Lilith?"

He rubbed his face with his two hands, then stared at them, one palm at a time. "Because I . . . Because I took both Ernest and Pat at the same time. She thought she was going to a slimming clinic, but actually she was going to a private mental institution. They notified me last night that she had escaped."

Dehan growled, "What mental institution?"

He shook his head. "I can't tell you."

She scowled at him. "Excuse me?"

He wouldn't meet her eye. "I am sorry, but I cannot tell you what clinic she was at."

"Why the hell not?"

"Because I am not prepared to betray her. If you get your hands on her, you will send her to some women's prison where they will torture her and do unthinkable things to her. I won't let that happen. She needs the protection of a good, private clinic. They are looking for her as we speak. They will find her and take her back, and if you want to know the name of the clinic, then I am afraid you will need a court order."

Dehan stared at me. I shrugged. She turned back to Cyril.

"You are willfully obstructing the course of justice and concealing evidence in a homicide investigation. You could go to prison for a very long time, Mr. Perkins."

"I beg to differ. I view the information you are requesting as being privileged. That information which is *not* privileged is a matter of public record. I suggest you contact the California health authorities and find out through them where my wife was hospitalized. Either that, or get a court order compelling me to give you what information I have."

"Very well, Mr. Perkins, we'll do that."

I stood for a moment, with my arms crossed over my chest, staring down at the floor.

"There is just one thing I would like to know, Mr. Perkins, before we go."

"What now?"

"Where did you bury the dogs?"

SIXTEEN

He stood. The movement was strangely jerky. He strode across the room and stood bare inches from the door, immobile, then turned and frowned at me. His face essayed several expressions: an incredulous smile, outrage, incomprehension.

"What . . ." He said it, then faltered. "What possible bearing . . ." He raised his eyebrows and narrowed his eyes. "The *dogs*?"

"Pat's dogs," I said.

"Why? *Why?* We are talking about my wife. You are accusing my daughter . . . coming up with all these crackpot theories, just madness! And now, having resolved *nothing*, you ask me about the *dogs*! Can we please get back to the matter at hand. You are like a . . . a . . ." His hands were flying around. "A child who cannot focus or concentrate on the issue at hand. Your mind is wandering . . ." His breathing was heavy. "The issue at hand," he said again.

I spoke quietly. "The issue at hand is . . ."

He stepped forward so that his legs and half his torso were framed in the dull light from the street. His chest and his face were in shadow. His voice was strained, trying not to be shrill.

"The issue at hand is, where is my wife?"

"That's what I am hoping you will tell us. But didn't you say she was nowhere?"

"Well, exactly, because now that you have lost her . . . You need to go and find her. Look for her. Because now she has killed Ernest. And you need to go! *Go!* And stop asking stupid questions!"

Theresa stood and crossed the room to where he stood. I could see he was trembling. For a moment they were both framed in the shadow of the window. She held him for a second, whispering in his ear, then guided him back to the sofa. As he sat, she hunkered down in front of him.

"Dad, it's okay. Everything is going to be okay. We'll find Mom. You want some water?"

He nodded. His smile to his daughter was an ugly rictus, his teeth bared and his eyes wide. "Yes, yes, water, thank you, darling."

She crossed through the light from the window again and filled a paper cup from the cooler. I repeated, "Where are the dogs buried, Mr. Perkins?"

His voice was a dry rasp. "They were destroyed."

"What does that mean?"

"I can't remember. They were old and infirm. I took them to the vet and had them destroyed."

"What do you mean by 'destroyed'?"

Theresa was standing over him holding his paper cup of water, watching him. She said, "Dad?"

He looked up and reached for the water. She said, "They are buried in the garden. Don't you remember? It wasn't that long ago."

He waved his hands in little jerks, frowning, making a "Sh-sh-sh . . ." sound. "No, no, hush, honey. No, they were incinerated."

"No, Dad. They're by the plum tree, by the vegetable patch."

"No! I had them incinerated! Stop *contradicting* me!"

"Dad?"

He stood again, pushed past his daughter, and started pacing, breathing hard.

"Why can't you just *find* her? It isn't enough that I lose Lilith and Pat on the same night! It isn't enough that I have to confine Ernest to a clinic! It isn't enough that I have to *lose my entire family*! Now you too persecute me, hound me . . ." He started to laugh. "Hound! Like the dogs! That's funny! You have to see the humor!"

He laughed, and the laughter turned to sobs. He went down slowly into a squatting position. Theresa ran to him. There was something incongruous in the care with which she set the water on the floor beside him. Like not spilling the water was more important than his emotional collapse.

Then she put her arms around him and he went to pieces, sobbing violently into her shoulder, repeating over and over, "*Oh God . . . oh God, I can't take any more. Please stop . . .*"

Dehan gave me a "what the hell is going on?" look, then went and helped Theresa lift Cyril to his feet and walk him back to the sofa. The paper cup of water toppled and spilled onto the carpet, but nobody seemed to notice. When he was sitting, Theresa turned to me.

"You have to go. I don't know what you think you are going to achieve with this, but I can't let you continue to hound my father like this. He is clearly having a nervous breakdown."

I nodded a few times, then looked down at my feet.

"Who's your vet?"

There was absolute silence. I looked up. Theresa was staring at her father. He was looking at his open hands, and his lower lip was trembling. I repeated, "Who is your vet? I'll swing by in the morning and ask for the records of the cremation." I hunched my shoulders. "As we speak, I have an officer making inquiries of all the vets in the area. It's a matter of time."

"Dad . . . ?"

I rested my ass on the edge of the desk and watched him. He

didn't answer. After a moment I said, "Why don't you tell us what really happened that night, Cyril?"

He was quiet so long I thought he wasn't going to answer. I glanced at Dehan, wondering whether we should take them both in. Then he spoke suddenly, and his voice was loud, almost shocking in the gloom.

"She went crazy at midday, as I told you. Ernest and I had been visiting with the Joneses. Gwen and Lilith, always so charming, sweet, and generous. A happy family." He looked up at me, like he was appealing to me for something. His cheeks were wet. "They had their tensions and disagreements, like any family," he said. "But they were solid, strong, loved each other. All they needed was a man. A quiet, stable, strong man."

"Like you."

"Well, why not? I am strong." He laughed. "My Lord! You have no idea how strong I can be! Eh, Theresa? How strong have we been over the years, in the face of unimaginable adversity?"

She spoke into the shadows. "Very strong, Daddy."

"I could have been a good husband. A stabilizing influence. I could have put her back on the right path. Eh, Theresa?"

"Yes, Daddy."

I said, "But Pat came and dragged you all home."

"Yes. She didn't know. Nobody knew, what I had prepared. It was a total Christmas surprise."

"What was the surprise, Cyril?"

"It was Theresa who gave me the idea." He smiled at her. "When she suggested that Ernest would be happier in a home. She knew we could afford it. We had no secrets, me and Theresa. She knew about my first wife. Didn't you, honey? We used it to get you through college, to get this surgery . . ."

I feared he would start rambling again, so I cut him short. "What idea, Cyril?"

"The clinic in California. Pat was not happy. She was always dreaming about California, Bobby Hansen . . . I knew she'd had sordid affairs. There are men who are attracted to women like her.

I was, once. So she went on her little holidays and did what she did. I knew that she fantasized about moving there with one of those beach bums, but I also knew her fantasies would never come to anything. It would be a blessing if they did, but they never would. So I had the idea of the clinic. A year, on the pretext of losing weight, tell her it was a two-week spa vacation. But really I would have her certified, and they would just keep her there, and give us some peace . . ."

He began to sob again. Theresa had gone very still. Her voice was almost a whisper.

"Daddy, you can't do that . . ."

"Pulling strings," he said into his hands. His voice was growing shrill again. "Pulling strings, like you did for Ernest. I know people, I can talk to people."

I raised my voice. "Stop it, Cyril. You can't pay to have a person certified. There is a procedure, it has to go before a judge. You can't just pay to have a person locked away."

He ignored me and went on. "After luncheon I presented her with an envelope, and inside it was the glossy leaflet showing a luxury retreat, with a spa, and lots of handsome, half-naked young men." His face twisted into a bitter mask. "She could hardly wait to get away. So I told her I would drive her that very evening to JFK to catch her flight out to Los Angeles . . ."

Theresa was shaking her head. "Daddy! *Daddy!* Stop it! You're scaring me. That's not possible!"

I interrupted her. "That was over lunch, you told her this?"

"After lunch, over dessert."

"What was on the menu for lunch?"

"What?"

"On the menu, for lunch?"

He blinked, momentarily confused. "Oh, the usual, turkey . . ."

"She prepared practically everything. You were at the Joneses', remember? But you made a salad, right?"

He nodded. "Oh, yes, you're right. I did make the salad."

"She loved it, right?"

"Yes, she did. She ate it all."

"And then you told her all about the luxury holiday."

"Yes, her and Ernest. They were captivated, and both very excited."

"So what happened next?"

"Well." He thought for a moment. "Then, I uh . . . she . . ." He looked up at the ceiling, swallowing hard. "We drove together to drop Ernest off. And that must be how she knew where he was. And then it was getting late, so I said I would get a cab back to the house and she should take the car to the airport."

"Why didn't you go to the airport with her?"

"Because I was worried. I realized I had left the fire burning in the grate. So she went off in the car, to the airport . . ."

"With the tickets."

"Yes, of course, I gave her the tickets."

"Why didn't you tell this to the investigating officer right at the start? Why did you lie and allow your wife to become the prime suspect in a murder investigation?"

He shrugged. "I panicked. I realized straightaway that we would both become suspects. I knew there was practically nil chance you would track her down at the clinic, and it was simple enough to go, collect the car, and dump it at Hunts Point, near Ernest's old place. It was probably stolen, repainted, and replated within hours."

"I'll say this for you, Cyril." I gave a small laugh. "You think fast on your feet. But I have to be honest with you. That is the biggest crock of bullshit I have ever heard in my life."

He shook his head. "No."

"You want to tell me, then, why Pat has escaped from her clinic and murdered her brother and Mary O'Connor? You want to explain to me how she even knows who Mary O'Connor is? And while you're at it, maybe you can explain why you said that you had 'lost' Lilith and your wife on the same night."

He screamed. He tore at his hair and he screamed, got to his feet, and pranced around the room tearing at his hair and drawing his nails over his face.

"All right! All right! All right! She fucking murdered Lilith! And I saw her do it! I saw her fucking murder Lilith!"

I waited. He was staring at me, his face flushed, his neck corded, and his fists clenched by his side. Suddenly he screamed again, *"And that makes me an accomplice!"* He started sobbing violently and raised a hand to point at Theresa. "She threatened our daughter."

Theresa shook her head. "What are you talking about, Dad? You have to stop this . . ."

"She knew about you and Lilith! I was clearing the table after lunch. She was in the living room, glued to the window. I went in to ask her if she wanted some cake. May God forgive me, I didn't notice the sewing basket on the table. She had the drapes open and the lights off. I asked her what she thought she was doing. She didn't answer. Then, over her shoulder, I saw Lilith walking quickly down the road toward her house. Pat hissed something and rushed to the door. Next thing, through the window I saw her rush up behind Lilith, and she just seemed to sort of pound her back. Lilith went down, on her face. I was paralyzed. Pat was just standing there. I could see big plumes of condensation around her head. It was bizarre. Then I ran out after her, and as I came up, it was like I said. It might have been a big dog, or a sack of wool lying there. Something impersonal and unreal."

He turned from his daughter to me.

"I dragged Pat inside, away from that horrible sight. My head was reeling. I told her I would have to call the police. She said that if I did she would frame Theresa. She knew that Theresa was having an affair with Lilith. She had seen them together, followed them to a hotel where they used to meet on Long Beach. That even if she was convicted, Theresa would be dragged through the mud, her career would be in ruins, her marriage . . . she would never survive. So I panicked. I made a call to a friend in San Francisco, a psychiatrist . . ."

"Who?"

He shook his head. "I can't tell you that. But she has been in his charge ever since."

I went back to the window and looked out. Darkness had closed in. Amber lights filtered through sleet that had turned to snow and was drifting against parked cars and facades, lampposts and hydrants. Over my shoulder I could hear Theresa saying, "How could Mom possibly have known about that, Dad?"

"She was obsessed. She watched Lilith all the time. She was so jealous. She saw you hanging out all the time, when you weren't at work you were with her, and when you were *at* work you were with her, driving her here and there like a taxi service. She became suspicious. Lilith was so . . . *servile* with you. She hung on your every word, was always *there* when you were around. I mean . . ." He laughed. "I was like an uncle. I had known her literally since you both were born. I was *there* for them both, taking care of them even though they weren't my family. But the one she was *fixated* on was you . . ."

I scratched my chin, shifted my gaze from Theresa to him. "And how would Pat have known that, Cyril?"

"You don't know her. She was always at the window, watching, listening . . ."

"Stop!"

His words trailed away.

"It's over, Cyril."

My cell rang, and I pulled it from my pocket. It was Joe, from the lab.

"Stone, you were right about the driver's license in Pat Perkins' name. There were prints all over it, but they were all either Patricia Perkins' or Mary O'Connor's, nobody else's. And preliminaries on the donuts show massive amounts of hemlock. Off the record, Ernest and Mary O'Connor were poisoned with hemlock. Frank will confirm that in his report, obviously, but that's what he's going to find."

"Thanks, Joe."

I hung up and stood looking at the phone for a while.

"Cyril, your brother-in-law, Ernest, and the woman who abducted him, posing as your wife, were both killed with massive doses of hemlock. Are you prepared to tell the truth now?"

"I've told you the truth. Pat killed Lilith. I should have come forward, I know, but the whole thing devastated me, and I had to protect my daughter. I . . ."

"Shut up, Cyril. Sit down and listen, and let me tell you what happened."

SEVENTEEN

"You're a good liar, Cyril, and like all good liars you stick to the truth as far as you can."

It had grown fully dark outside, but nobody had switched on the lights. The only light there was came from the streetlamps outside the window, and the warm glow of Theresa's desk lamp. Cyril was sitting hunched on the sofa. I could see the pale oval of his face turned toward me, but I could barely make out his expression.

"Ern did go to visit Gwen Jones in the midmorning. We know that from Gwen herself. And then you went and joined him. But we also know that you were not there for Gwen. She told us herself that she spent all the time in the kitchen while you and your brother-in-law lavished your attention on Lilith." I smiled and gave a small snort. "You were as infatuated with Lilith as Ern was. In fact, I think it was more than infatuation. I think you had become steadily more obsessed with her as you had watched her grow from a teenager into a young woman. And that obsession was stoked and fanned by the years of pain and servitude that you suffered at the hands of your wife. The more she harangued you, beat you, and nagged you, the more she slandered Lilith, the more you sought refuge in her and fostered your dreams about her.

What did you think, Cyril? That, having lost her father, she would develop 'daddy issues' over you?"

I saw his head drop forward and heard the stifled choke of a sob.

I sighed and shook my head. "What I don't understand is, if things were so bad with Pat, why didn't you just divorce her and leave?"

He didn't answer for a moment. Then he dragged a sleeve across his face and said, "I'm a Catholic. And besides, there was the risk that she would win custody, and I would have to leave Theresa with her. That was never going to happen."

"So you suffered, for over twenty years, pretending that you loved her, tolerating her violence and . . ."

I hesitated, but he filled in the blanks. "Her stupidity and her sadism."

"But you're a man who fixes problems. That's right, isn't it, Cyril? You don't hang around hoping things will get better. You see a problem, and you fix it. It might take more or less time, but sooner or later, you find a solution. And, two gets you twenty, when Lilith turned eighteen you started to formulate a plan. First, the more she stopped to chat with you, the more she was willing to spend time drinking coffee with you and listening to you talk, laughing at your witticisms, the more you allowed yourself to believe the fantasy that she was falling for you. That you stood a chance with her. And the more that thought grew in your mind, the more you were aware of the immovable nature of the obstacle: your wife.

"Somehow she had to go. Somehow you had to get rid of her. But how?

"You explored the possibility of having her committed. You looked into the legislation and realized there would have to be a court hearing, and you could only have her put away if she had serious mental health issues. But she didn't. She was just stupid and malicious, not crazy.

"And by the time Theresa was old enough to start making a

life of her own, divorce became a possibility again, but it was a possibility you could not contemplate, because Pat would have a claim to at least half of all your assets, and that would leave you unable to help Theresa as you had been, and it would also expose the two million dollars you had extorted from the insurance company to a possible investigation, and *that* was something you could not risk. So that left you with only one option. Pat had to die. And after more than twenty years of suffering at her hands, I am guessing that was not such a hard decision to make.

"So, being a thorough, methodical man with an academic bent, you began to investigate your options, and I am willing to bet it did not take you long to settle on hemlock."

He sank back in the sofa so his face was in shadow. His voice was sullen and harsh. "There was an exquisite irony to the fact that the stupidest, basest woman in the world should die the same way as Socrates."

"There was also the fact that there would be no violent thrashing around, no foaming at the mouth, just a steady, quiet paralysis. And, above all, she could die while you were not there, and you could provide yourself with a nice, solid alibi for the time of Lilith's death and Pat's disappearance.

"So, while Ern was flirting with Lilith and Pat was slaving over a hot stove, you set about preparing your wife a delicious salad with hemlock leaves. What did you do, grow it in the garden? I wonder what you told her it was? Parsley? It has a mild, parsnip-like taste. With a good dressing . . ."

Again the bitter, twisted voice from the shadows: "With her appetite she would eat anything. I sat and watched her stuffing forkful after forkful into her mouth, knowing that within just a couple of hours she would be dead."

I glanced at Dehan. She gave an imperceptible shake of the head. It would not stand as a confession. I pressed on.

"So, after half an hour, when you saw it starting to take effect, you took Ern and told him it was time to move him into his new home. You put him in the car and delivered him to Dr. Fraser's clinic in Ardsley-on-Hudson. Then you drove back, where to? Hunts Point, as you just suggested? Or had you rented a lockup somewhere?"

He nodded. "Both. I rented a lockup in Hunts Point. The car has been sitting there since that night. I'd left my own car there earlier and drove it back."

"On Christmas Day at that time in the evening, the whole thing couldn't have taken more than a couple of hours or less. You were probably back by six thirty or seven. What I am not sure about is how you knew so precisely what time Lilith would be returning from her supposed visit to Mrs. Rodriguez."

He was quiet. I was about to go on, but he cut me short.

"That wasn't so difficult. I knew Theresa and Lilith were having an affair. I was not infatuated with Lilith, or obsessed, Detective Stone. I was quite simply in love with her. I felt my heart break day by day as that awful realization dawned on me, that her lack of interest in boys was not because she was infatuated with me, but because she was in love with my daughter. It was hard to believe and harder to accept, so I took to following them, and I saw them go to that awful, seedy place." He turned to look at his daughter. "How could you?"

She stood and walked away from him. "How could I, Dad? How could *you*?"

He ignored her and went on. "Lilith had taken to talking about a boyfriend. I knew there was no boyfriend. I knew who it was, but I played along.

"I knew that every Christmas Day she took some food to Mrs. Rodriguez, so on that day I waited in the front yard with the pretext of smoking my pipe. As she passed, I engaged her in conversation, as I had done so many times before, and asked, one conspirator to another, if she was going to meet with her boyfriend.

"I knew what her answer would be. Theresa had already told me she would be meeting up with Lilith that evening for a couple of hours. That was her reason for not coming over to see us. So it was a cinch. I told Lilith I would drop in for a visit with Gwen and entertain her till eight while Pat slept off her luncheon. It was an unspoken understanding by then between Theresa, Lilith, and myself that Gwen and I were a potential item. So she was only too happy to oblige." He paused and looked at Theresa. "If you'd had the faintest idea of how that little game drove a knife into my heart day after day, pretending it was Gwen I liked when my heart was breaking for Lilith." He sighed. "But to answer your question, Detective, it was not difficult to fix it so Lilith would return at just before eight."

The full horror of what this meant was only just beginning to dawn on Theresa. She turned in three slow, clumsy steps to face her father, and slowly her hands went to cover her mouth.

I spoke, watching her. "I imagine that you used a sheet or a blanket to drag Pat to the cellar . . ."

"The wheelbarrow. I had cleaned the wheel, so it left no trace on the carpet. I opened the door and tipped her down the stairs. Then took her scissors from the sewing basket and waited for Lilith to appear, walking down the sidewalk. I slipped out and stayed in the shadows. There is only one streetlamp on that stretch of road. And . . ." He shrugged. "It was surprisingly easy, after the way she had betrayed me after all those years, after the way she had hurt me and destroyed my heart, after everything she had done. As she walked past, I stepped up behind her and stabbed the fucking little whore in the back."

There was a small gasping noise, and Theresa swayed and fell with a loud slam on the floor. Cyril stood, with hesitant steps. I pointed to a chair and snapped, "Sit down!"

He sat, and between us, Dehan and I lifted Theresa onto the sofa. Dehan got some water and started patting it onto her face. I turned to Cyril.

"You left no prints on the scissors. I'm guessing Theresa kept Pat supplied with surgical gloves."

"The scissors, her driver's license, her cell, her credit card. I cleaned them all and then carefully pressed her prints onto them, just in case I ever needed to use them."

I nodded. "Yeah, too thorough. It would have been less suspicious if her driver's license had had all the prints you expect to see on that kind of card, instead of only hers and Mary O'Connor's."

"I guess I panicked."

"Yeah, and you panicked again when we started investigating it as a cold case. That was what made you set up that stupid charade with Mary O'Connor. You were scared that Ern would say something about Christmas that would put us on the right track. I figure you were also scared that I suspected Pat had been murdered. So you decided to prove she was alive and well by having her abduct Ern and poison him, thus killing two birds with one stone. But you forgot to tell Mary to use gloves at all times, and that was when your plan started to unravel."

Theresa had come 'round. She gave a small cry and started to sob. Dehan looked over at Cyril and then at me.

She said, "But there is something I don't get. Okay, I get the use of hemlock so you could establish an alibi at Fraser's clinic, because hemlock is slow acting but paralysis sets in early on, and having Pat disappear, she automatically becomes the focus of the investigation into Lilith's murder. But what I don't get is, where's the body? From the start we discounted Pat's murder as an explanation for her disappearance precisely because a body is hard to dispose of, especially a large body like Pat Perkins'. You didn't bury her, or the cops and your neighbors would have noticed your backyard was a mess. You didn't dump her in the river, you couldn't. A, she would float and B, getting a body that heavy into the water is very, very difficult. Besides, you simply didn't have time! You called the cops that very night. Also, you just said you dumped her into the cellar, and getting her out again would have required a crane. So, where the hell is she? And also, how did her hair wind up in Ern's fingers?"

I turned to Cyril. He was silent, like he wasn't going to answer.

I said, "You didn't dispose of her, did you? At least, not exactly. You let the dogs do it for you, didn't you?"

He smiled. "That was very perceptive of you, Detective Stone."

"You put them in the cellar with her and you didn't feed them. You took them out at their appointed time every day, and then you brought them back again and put them back in the cellar. Unlike cats, dogs do not know when they have eaten enough. They will eat as much as you feed them and just keep going. I don't know how long it took, but I can't imagine it took more than a week, by which time your dogs would have been bloated and infirm."

He gave a small, strange laugh. Theresa had curled up into the fetal position and was covering her ears, sobbing softly. Cyril spoke in a strange voice, like he was half-absent.

"The poor dogs couldn't cope entirely on their own. I made a few stews, even had some myself. Mostly I took them down to the mission. I felt it was right she should give back to a world she had taken so much from."

Dehan shook her head. "Jesus! You *ate* her?"

"Mainly the dogs did, but I helped, and so did the community she despised so much."

Theresa just kept repeating, "*Dad, no, no, please Dad, no . . .*" over and over. I said, "You'd better call her doctor. She needs a sedative."

Cyril spoke suddenly, in a loud, clear voice. "You'll never prove any of this. I'll deny it. I'll say you did all the talking and browbeat these two into believing it. It is too far-fetched. It's madness. None of this happened. I'll get the best attorney. You will never prove it. Not in a million years."

"Dehan and I are both witnesses. Theresa heard you too."

"Nobody trusts the police, and Theresa is totally unreliable as a witness. She is overemotional and damaged by her mother's betrayal. You have no forensic evidence, and without that your case is nothing." He gave a bark of a laugh. "Habeas corpus!"

I stepped over to him and looked deep into his cold, crazy eyes.

"Cyril Perkins, I am placing you under arrest for the murder of Lilith Jones and your wife, Patricia Perkins. You have the right to remain silent, but anything you do say may and will be taken down and used against you in a court of law. You have the right to an attorney. If you don't have one . . ."

"I have one, and he will tear your case apart, Detective Stone, and blow it in your face."

Dehan cuffed him and sat him down, then called for a doctor to come and see Theresa. Meanwhile I called Dispatch and had them send a couple of patrol cars and the crime scene team to Perkins' house. After that I called Joe and put it on speaker. I sat with my ass on the desk and watched Perkins as it rang.

"Yeah, Stone, it's Joe. We're on our way. What can I do for you?"

"It's an unusual case, Joe. We have a confession of a double murder, and cannibalism on one of the victims, but then that confession has been retracted."

"Oh, that sucks. What do you want from me?"

"Bear with me, Joe. The victim who was eaten was largely eaten by her dogs. And the dogs are buried in the backyard. They have been there less than a year, so you may be able to recover something from the digestive tract."

"If they died soon after eating, it's possible."

"Good, but I'd like you to leave that to your team and come over to the surgery of the accused's daughter."

"A medical surgery?"

"Yeah, and there is one item in particular I would like you to examine very, very carefully."

"Yeah, what's that?"

"Well, you see, Mr. Perkins and his two dogs disposed of all the flesh—some two hundred and forty or fifty pounds of it—but then he was left with all the bones. How the hell do you dispose of an entire human skeleton without attracting attention?"

"It's not easy."

Cyril was watching me. As I spoke, he closed his eyes.

"So, Joe, what I would like you to do is to examine the skeleton that Theresa Perkins has hanging in her surgery, and see if you can't get a DNA profile from it. I think we may finally have found what is left of Patricia Perkins."

EPILOGUE

THE TREE SPARKLED LIKE A BADLY WRAPPED CHRISTMAS present, the way trees are supposed to sparkle. The angel at the top stared at the ceiling, and I told myself her look was not so much manic as full of divine grace.

On my new record player, a vinyl spun to the tune of "The Holly and the Ivy." For a moment they seemed to sing, "Oh the hemlock and the ivy, when they are both full grown . . . !" But I put the thought from my mind.

Dehan pulled the drapes across the black glass of the window and sat in the armchair by the tree, watching me where I stood at the mantelpiece. I raised the martini she had just given me, and she raised her own in reply.

"Merry Christmas Eve, Mrs. Stone."

"Merry Christmas Eve, Mr. Stone. How long till Christmas?"

"Why?"

"I want to give you your present."

I looked at my watch. "Half an hour, but we should wait till tomorrow morning."

"I plan to be doing something else tomorrow morning."

"Making Christmas breakfast?"

"Yeah, that."

She went quiet for a moment, then said, "Stone, explain something to me."

"Well," I said, facetiously, "you know the little bunny wabbits, the birds and the bees . . . ?"

"Shut up, I'm serious. When did you first realize that Pat had been murdered?"

I shrugged. "Pretty much when we took the case. Before that. It was the only explanation that made sense. I didn't *know*, but I figured. What I couldn't get, like you, was who dunnit and what the hell they'd done with the body. Then, when we'd narrowed it down to either Theresa or Cyril, the absence of the dogs suggested a solution. And, you remember when we were in the Jacobi parking lot, and I suddenly said, 'The surgery!' and you thought I was afraid for Theresa's life?"

"Yeah. You mean you weren't?"

"No. I had just remembered her skeleton hanging in the corner. Then the whole thing made sense. It was just a question of nailing down which one of them killed her. My money was on Cyril."

"Why? Theresa had just as strong a motive."

"Yeah, but if she was going to poison somebody, she would have used chemicals. Hemlock is a gardener's poison."

She frowned at me. "What makes you think Cyril is a gardener?"

I laughed. "Did you see those slippers he was wearing? Any man who wears slippers like that potters in the garden. Besides, when I looked out of his window that first day, he had a vegetable patch. I knew he was a gardener, so my money was on him."

The clock in the kitchen struck twelve, and we smiled at each other. She rose and went to the tree, from which she took a long, thick envelope bound with a gold ribbon. She gave me a kiss and handed it to me.

"Merry Christmas, you hunk of beef, you."

I kissed her back and gently groped the envelope while I did it. It felt just like two tickets to Hawaii.

Don't miss MOMMY'S LITTLE KILLER. The riveting sequel in the Dead Cold Mystery series.

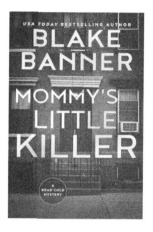

Scan the QR code below to purchase MOMMY'S LITTLE KILLER.

Or go to: righthouse.com/mommys-little-killer

NOTE: flip to the very end to read an exclusive sneak peak...

DON'T MISS ANYTHING!

If you want to stay up to date on all new releases in this series, with this author, or with any of our new deals, you can do so by joining our newsletters below.

In addition, you will immediately gain access to our entire *Right House VIP Library,* which includes many riveting Mystery and Thriller novels for your enjoyment!

righthouse.com/email

(Easy to unsubscribe. No spam. Ever.)

ALSO BY BLAKE BANNER

Up to date books can be found at:
www.righthouse.com/blake-banner

ROGUE THRILLERS
Gates of Hell (Book 1)
Hell's Fury (Book 2)

ALEX MASON THRILLERS
Odin (Book 1)
Ice Cold Spy (Book 2)
Mason's Law (Book 3)
Assets and Liabilities (Book 4)
Russian Roulette (Book 5)
Executive Order (Book 6)
Dead Man Talking (Book 7)
All The King's Men (Book 8)
Flashpoint (Book 9)
Brotherhood of the Goat (Book 10)
Dead Hot (Book 11)
Blood on Megiddo (Book 12)
Son of Hell (Book 13)

HARRY BAUER THRILLER SERIES
Dead of Night (Book 1)
Dying Breath (Book 2)
The Einstaat Brief (Book 3)
Quantum Kill (Book 4)
Immortal Hate (Book 5)
The Silent Blade (Book 6)
LA: Wild Justice (Book 7)

Breath of Hell (Book 8)
Invisible Evil (Book 9)
The Shadow of Ukupacha (Book 10)
Sweet Razor Cut (Book 11)
Blood of the Innocent (Book 12)
Blood on Balthazar (Book 13)
Simple Kill (Book 14)
Riding The Devil (Book 15)
The Unavenged (Book 16)
The Devil's Vengeance (Book 17)
Bloody Retribution (Book 18)
Rogue Kill (Book 19)
Blood for Blood (Book 20)

DEAD COLD MYSTERY SERIES
An Ace and a Pair (Book 1)
Two Bare Arms (Book 2)
Garden of the Damned (Book 3)
Let Us Prey (Book 4)
The Sins of the Father (Book 5)
Strange and Sinister Path (Book 6)
The Heart to Kill (Book 7)
Unnatural Murder (Book 8)
Fire from Heaven (Book 9)
To Kill Upon A Kiss (Book 10)
Murder Most Scottish (Book 11)
The Butcher of Whitechapel (Book 12)
Little Dead Riding Hood (Book 13)
Trick or Treat (Book 14)
Blood Into Wine (Book 15)
Jack In The Box (Book 16)
The Fall Moon (Book 17)
Blood In Babylon (Book 18)
Death In Dexter (Book 19)
Mustang Sally (Book 20)

A Christmas Killing (Book 21)
Mommy's Little Killer (Book 22)
Bleed Out (Book 23)
Dead and Buried (Book 24)
In Hot Blood (Book 25)
Fallen Angels (Book 26)
Knife Edge (Book 27)
Along Came A Spider (Book 28)
Cold Blood (Book 29)
Curtain Call (Book 30)

THE OMEGA SERIES
Dawn of the Hunter (Book 1)
Double Edged Blade (Book 2)
The Storm (Book 3)
The Hand of War (Book 4)
A Harvest of Blood (Book 5)
To Rule in Hell (Book 6)
Kill: One (Book 7)
Powder Burn (Book 8)
Kill: Two (Book 9)
Unleashed (Book 10)
The Omicron Kill (Book 11)
9mm Justice (Book 12)
Kill: Four (Book 13)
Death In Freedom (Book 14)
Endgame (Book 15)

ABOUT US

Right House is an independent publisher created by authors for readers. We specialize in Action, Thriller, Mystery, and Crime novels.

If you enjoyed this novel, then there is a good chance you will like what else we have to offer! Please stay up to date by using any of the links below.

Join our mailing lists to stay up to date -->
righthouse.com/email
Visit our website --> righthouse.com
Contact us --> contact@righthouse.com

facebook.com/righthousebooks
x.com/righthousebooks
instagram.com/righthousebooks

EXCLUSIVE SNEAK PEAK OF...

MOMMY'S LITTLE KILLER

CHAPTER 1

"John—"

"Sir—"

"Twenty-one sixty-one Watson Avenue. A woman has been murdered, and I want you and Dehan to take lead."

I took a moment to scratch my ear, then said, "Sir?"

A tiny sigh at the other end of the line and the chief said, "Do I really need to repeat it, John?"

"No, sir, twenty-one sixty-one Watson Avenue, a woman has been murdered. You want us to lead. We'll go right away."

"When you're done, come and see me straightaway. It's four fifteen. I'll expect you before six."

"Yes, sir."

I hung up. Dehan had been examining the eraser on her pencil and now shifted her narrowed eyes and pensively pursed lips in my direction. Her face was a question, so I said, "We have a live, active, hot case, Dehan, where the evidence is as fresh as dew-kissed March tulips. Let us not waste a moment!"

She stood and pulled on her black leather jacket while I shrugged into my coat, and as we headed out of the station and trotted down the two shallow steps toward my ancient burgundy Jaguar, she said:

"A woman, apparently murdered in her home, just south of the Cross Bronx Expressway . . ."

"Twenty-one sixty-one, that places it near the overpass, by the Westchester Creek."

"And the chief wants us to take lead because . . . ?"

I opened the driver's door and climbed in. She got in the other side, and the doors slammed like two gunshots. The big cat growled into life, and I reversed out of the lot.

"He didn't say. He just said he wants us to report to him as soon as we're done at the victim's house."

"So, either the case is important because the president's bill-fold was found at the scene, and only we are good enough to deal with such a sensitive case; he's taking us off cold cases and putting us on hot ones; or this case relates somehow to a cold case and he figures we may as well take it and kill however many birds with one stone."

"My money is on that one."

I pulled onto the Bruckner Boulevard and began to accelerate. Dehan was beating a tattoo on her knees.

"So, it's an MO we've seen before in one of the cold cases."

I glanced at her and frowned. "We'll be there in five minutes and we'll find out."

"There is nothing wrong, Stone, with exercising one's deductive faculties by attempting to anticipate what one is going to find in any given situation . . ."

"Dear me . . ."

". . . or set of circumstances. Call it an intellectual workout."

"Fair enough."

"At this early stage of the investigation it is unlikely to be a weapon, or a suspect, or indeed a victim. What is far more likely is that it is an MO we have seen in a previous case or cases."

I smiled at her and the slightly pompous language she was using. "Makes sense."

"We can, my dear Stone, extrapolate a little further. For a

modus operandi to stick in the chief's memory to the point that he would call us in for a renewed offense, we are looking at two things: that the MO was used a number of times and the perp is therefore a serial offender, and that it is a very serious crime—as murder indeed is."

I arched both of my eyebrows very high. "A serial killer, Dehan? That is one hell of a leap."

She spread her hands and thrust out her bottom lip. "Well, now you can gloat when you prove me wrong, can't you, Mr. Stone."

Then she grinned at me and winked and I felt odd and wobbly inside. She could still do that.

I turned left onto Castle Hill and after two blocks turned onto Blackrock Avenue, to enter Watson from the west. The house was opposite the Catholic Church of the Holy Family. There were two patrol cars outside, a crime scene van, and Frank the ME's mid-'90s Jeep Cherokee. There were also a couple of uniforms, a sergeant, and a lot of tape.

I pulled up next to Frank's Jeep and we climbed out. The sky was a clear, pallid blue, but there was already the ghost of a translucent silver moon drifting above the rooftops. A chill breeze crept in and made my skin crawl. Dehan shuddered and stuffed her hands in her pockets.

The sergeant knew us and lifted the tape. He had grizzled hair turning to gray and eyes that were slightly yellow where they should be white. He didn't look surprised to see us. But then he looked like there were few things left on Earth that would surprise him. His greeting was terse.

"Detectives."

"Sergeant Musa, who called it in?"

"Benny Jackson. He's inside. He didn't exactly call it in. More like he lost his shit and went screaming to the next-door neighbor, and she called it in. A Ms. Edna Brown."

Dehan asked, "Has he said what he was doing here?"

He shook his head. "But Edna says he was a frequent visitor."

I gave a single nod that I understood the euphemism and turned to Dehan. "Okay, let's go have a look."

Sergeant Musa turned away. "It ain't pretty."

We climbed the six steps to the front porch of the two-story redbrick box. My feet were heavy, and my legs were reluctant to move. Death is unpleasant to see. Murder is horror, madness, turned banal. Dehan glanced at me, took a deep breath, and stepped through the door like a woman diving into a cold pool in January.

The entrance hall was small, no more than seven feet square, with a narrow staircase carpeted in deep burgundy climbing up the left wall, and a white door open on the right. Through it I saw a man sitting on a faded red sofa with his elbows on his knees. He was big, tall, and lean, with big hands and feet. He had dark skin and tightly curled hair, with a scraggy beard. He watched me with large, frightened eyes.

There was a uniformed cop on the door. She had the pallor of someone who has recently vomited. She jerked her head at the stairs. "In the bedroom . . ." She winced and gave her head a small shake.

I led the way up on heavy feet. A guy in a plastic suit was dusting the banisters for prints. At the top there was a small landing, also carpeted in deep burgundy. There were three doors. The one at the far end stood open and gave onto a bathroom. The walls gleamed white under a fluorescent bulb that was reflected in a partially visible mirror. The door on the left was also open, though the light was off and the drapes were closed. From the posters I could make out on the walls, the football on the chest of drawers, and the jacket hanging on the back of the chair, I figured it might be a boy's room, though it may have been a person of gender fluidity who self-identified as a boy. In a world where everything is anything, who could tell?

The door directly in front was also open. The room was full of people, all of them dressed like spacemen in hazard suits, moving slowly around a large bed. Some were crouched down, examining the floor, while others were standing, inspecting the headboard, the bedside tables, and the wardrobe.

We stepped through the doorway into insanity. On the floor, beside the bed, I noticed a small pile of discarded clothes. The bed itself appeared at first glance to have red sheets. But it was no ordinary dye that made it that color. The sheet, the duvet, and large parts of the pillows were saturated with thick blood. Lying on the sodden sheet, with the duvet tangled around her feet and legs, was a woman. Or, more accurately, what was left of a woman.

At a guess she was in her forties, on the plump side. She lay naked, her peroxide hair tangled on the soaked red pillow. Her eyes were wide with terror, staring at a ceiling that was speckled with blood. Her mouth was open. Her arms were straight down by her sides and her fingers had clawed so hard at the sheets, she had torn into the mattress beneath.

Both breasts had been removed and lay deflated and grotesque on either side of her head. A large hunting knife with a black rubber handle protruded from her lower abdomen, just above her pubic bone. Her face, at first horrific in its expression of abject terror, had been painted with a thick coat of very red lipstick and blue eyeshadow.

Frank, slightly stooped, was leaning over her, but watching us.

I heard a sniffing from beside me and turned to look at Dehan. She said:

"Lavender. Essential oil of lavender."

Frank said, "Good." Then he straightened up and stepped toward the door. "Please leave. The scene is rich. It's hard enough for us not to disturb things, and we know what we're doing."

"Rich?" I stepped closer to the head of the bed, taking care not to tread in the blood that had spilled there. I studied the twisted, agonized expression, and the exquisitely clean cut to the breast. "I don't think you're going to find a single trace of forensic evidence."

He ignored me.

"Joe's down in the kitchen. Looks like they may have been in the kitchen together having a drink or a cup of coffee before they came up here." He paused, glanced at us both in turn, and added, "I'm not that surprised to see you, to be honest. I thought the inspector might send you. I called him."

I nodded. "I can see why."

Dehan said, "The lavender, the knife in the womb, the boobs . . . What did they call him? Mommy's Boy?"

"Yeah. Five, six years ago?"

Frank stuck out his lower lip and gave his head a small shake. "It spanned a year, between 2014 and 2015. There were five that we know of, and I examined all of them. This was exactly his modus operandi. Then suddenly he just stopped."

Dehan grunted. "Looks like he just had a Kit Kat." She jerked her head at the body. "She was alive during the worst of it."

"I'm afraid so. I can tell you more when I get her back to the lab. But there are a couple of details . . ." He pointed back at the ghastly, raw wounds on her chest. "In the original killings he removed the left breast first, antemortem. As you can imagine this causes profound shock; the heart accelerates violently and the victim bleeds out very quickly. You can see there, the bleeding from the left breast is copious. However, when he removed the right breast, it was either perimortem or postmortem. There is practically no bleeding. And there is none from the knife wound."

I asked, "Who knew that, Frank? Was that ever in the news?"

He shook his head. "I knew that, my team knew, and Detective Alvarez and his team must have known, but it was never considered a fact of much relevance. Now, of course, it becomes one. The other point which might have just become relevant is the makeup."

I nodded. "I was going to talk to Joe about that . . ."

Dehan interrupted me. "We need that analyzed and compared with the makeup used in the original killings. Was it always the same?"

Frank smiled at her, but not with much humor. "Yes, that was my point. He always used the same brand and shades. L'Oréal—"

"Because she's worth it."

Frank glanced at her curiously, then went on, "All Night Blue, number six. The lipstick was British Red Three Fifty. The mascara was Age Perfect Lash Magnifying, with conditioning serum."

Dehan echoed my previous question. "And who would have known that?"

Frank shook his head. "Me, Joe, one or two guys on our teams, Alvarez. We discussed it, but the detective's attitude, and I can understand it, was that it was interesting, but it didn't really get you anywhere."

There was a derisive edge to Dehan's snort. "Well it will now. It will tell us if our perp's a copycat or the real thing."

I nodded. "And a little more than that, I hope. Frank, we'll come and see you when you have her at the lab. I want to see if Joe has anything downstairs."

Dehan led the way back down, speaking over her shoulder as she went. "In the Mommy's Boy murders they never found any forensic evidence at the scene. Alvarez never got close. Where is Alvarez now? He moved west, didn't he?"

"San Diego PD. He took a lot of flack for not solving the case."

The kitchen was part of an open-plan living room, dining room, kitchen affair with narrow French doors onto a backyard. The drapes were closed, like the drapes over the window that looked out onto Watson Avenue and the Holy Family Church. There was a small dining table down by the kitchen, with three bentwood chairs. And almost opposite the door there was a red sofa and a coffee table facing a large, flat-screen TV. Forming a nest with the sofa, there were two battered armchairs.

In and around the kitchen were Joe, the head of the crime scene team, and a couple of his guys, all dressed in plastic. On the sofa, watching us with big, frightened eyes, was the same guy I'd seen earlier. Sergeant Musa was with him, writing in a notebook. I approached.

"Benny Jackson?"

He nodded. "Yeah."

I sat in one of the armchairs, and Dehan remained standing, watching him. Musa closed his pad. "I'm done. You need me for anything?"

I told him I didn't, and he left. I said to Benny, "Tell me what happened."

He jerked his head at the door. "I just told him."

I allowed my mouth to pretend it was smiling. My eyes told him it wasn't for real. "Now tell me. As soon as you do that, you can go home."

"I come to see Claire, 'bout four o'clock. The door was open. I come in and I went upstairs . . ."

Dehan was already shaking her head. "Slow down, Benny. Let's start with how come you just went in when the door was open. You didn't knock or ring the bell?"

"No. We was friends. She often left the door open and I just come in. That weren't nothin' strange."

"Okay, so how come you didn't come in here to look for her, or the kitchen?"

He shrugged. "I called her. She din' answer, and sometimes, a lot of times, when I come to see her she's already upstairs in her room. So I just done like I always done. I went right on up."

Realization dawned. "You were having a sexual relationship with Claire?"

He screwed up his brow. "Huh?"

"You and Claire were lovers."

His slack mouth kind of sagged into a smile. "Lovers?" He grunted something like a laugh. "Yeah, right, lovers."

Dehan arched an eyebrow and folded her arms. "Are you saying she was a sex worker?"

"No, man, nothin' like that. She was a gas, we had a laugh.

Ain't nobody rich 'round here. We all need a bit of somethin', right? I give her fifty bucks sometimes and she says, come 'round, we'll have a party. That kinda thing. Claire weren't nobody's whore, man. She was a good woman. I'm gonna miss her bad."

His lips and his nose seemed to swell instantly, his eyes flooded with tears, and he wiped his whole face with his wrists.

Dehan spoke softly. "I'm sorry, Benny, I didn't know. It's gotta be tough."

He wiped his face with his sleeve now. "When I got up there and saw what I seen, I just kinda lost it. I didn't wanna see that, man, and I ran. I think I was screamin'. When I got to the front yard, Edna was on the porch saying, 'What happened? What happened? Benny, talk to me!' and I'm just screamin' like a crazy person, till I says to her, 'Call the cops, Edna! Call the cops. Claire's been hurt. She's been hurt real bad!' I din' wanna believe she was dead."

It was a simple enough story, and unless he was a thespian genius, he was telling the truth as accurately as he remembered it. I asked him, "Think carefully, Benny. When you were approaching the house, did you see anyone, did anything happen that caught your attention? Anything at all out of the ordinary?"

"Man, I was jus' thinkin' about Claire and her moves, and the party we was gonna have. I wasn't thinkin' about nothin' else. I din' see nobody nor nothin' strange at all."

Dehan said, "Cars."

He squinted at her. "What?"

"Cars. Most of the time the cars parked outside houses in residential areas are the same cars, in pretty much the same places at the same times." He thought about it a second and shrugged. She went on. "Think back. Were they the same cars?"

"Maybe . . ." He paused. "You know? Now you say it, maybe, there was an old-model cream Ford SUV, maybe a Kuga? Maybe, 'cross the way, outside the church."

I sucked my teeth for a moment, then sighed and nodded. "Okay, Benny. You can go. On your way out tell Sergeant Musa about the car so he can add it to your statement. Show him where you saw it."

He got to his feet and walked out of the room, rubbing the back of his head with his huge hand and sobbing quietly as he went.

CHAPTER 2

Joe had told us he would have nothing for us until he'd finished and got back to the lab, so we went next door to Edna Brown's house. Dusk was turning to evening and the cold air had developed an icy bite. Edna was at her bow window, peering through her drapes with the warm light of her living room behind her. When she saw us enter her front yard and climb the steps, she left the window and hurried to the door. It opened as Dehan reached for the bell.

"I saw yous coming," she said, and offered us an uncertain smile.

I offered her a certain one and said, "We saw you see us. May we come in?"

She stood back, and the light from her hall illuminated her face. She was in her seventies, with very white skin and pink cheeks. "Is it true? Is Claire dead?"

Dehan answered. "I'm afraid so, Edna. Can you tell us anything?"

Her house was the mirror of Claire's. We had the stairs on our right, and to the left there was a door open onto a cozy, well-kept living room. She didn't answer Dehan but turned her back and tottered away toward the living room, where a gold Dralon velvet sofa and two chairs set about a coffee table echoed the shabbier setup in Claire's house. She sat on the corner of the sofa and watched us take the chairs, with her hands placed neatly on her lap.

"Poor Claire. She did struggle so. It's a cruel, hard life in this country unless you are a ruthless predator. Bless her, Claire was anything but that. She had a big heart and a weak disposition." She closed her eyes and gave her head a single shake. "And a *chronic* need for cash."

Dehan shot me a smile. "What are you trying to tell us, Edna?"

Edna smiled at her and blinked a few times. "Please, call me Mrs. Brown. I do so despise the modern lack of formality, and unless I am very much mistaken, we have not been introduced before." She sailed on seamlessly. "I am not *trying* to tell you anything. It's quite simply that poor Claire had to make ends meet, and when faced with poverty most of us do what we are good at. Some of us invest in the stock market, others turn to hydroponics and grow marijuana in the basement, while others resort to the world's oldest profession and sell sexual favors to men who are too ugly to get them in the usual manner."

I gave a small laugh and decided that I liked Mrs. Brown. "Are you skilled in hydroponics, Mrs. Brown?"

She gave a charming giggle. "Oh, dear me! You'll need a court order to find that out, and as you are Homicide and not Vice, I doubt you'll bother. Besides, no judge in this city will grant one on the basis of my whimsical passing comment. What were we talking about? You want me to tell you what happened."

"Please."

She sighed and slipped her hands between her knees. "Benny was a frequent visitor at Claire's house. They were fond of each other. She wouldn't sleep with just anyone." She frowned and shook her head. "She wasn't what you'd call a *whore*, as such. She was a party animal. She *loved* to laugh and dance and sing. She could drink most people under the table and still dance a jig around the room without falling over. Many a New Year's Eve we have partied in her house and mine until the sun has risen on a brand-new January.

"And her customers were gleaned from her friends." She wagged a finger at us. "Not her acquaintances, mind! Her *friends*. And Benny, for all that he is an ignorant dopehead, he is also kind and sensitive, and he would remember to buy her flowers from time to time, and never had to be reminded that it was her birthday. So he knew that she was hard up, and he would give her one or two hundred dollars a month. In exchange he would visit her whenever his appetite got the better of his ED."

Dehan frowned. "ED?"

"Erectile dysfunction. In a man of Benny's age, who drinks and smokes as much as he does, a little soldier who stands to attention on demand is something between a forlorn hope and a distant memory."

She leaned back with her hands clamped tightly between her knees, her cheeks glowing bright pink against her white skin, and giggled silently with her eyes screwed up tight.

Dehan smiled at me and raised her eyebrows high. When Mrs. Brown had stopped giggling, she asked her, "Did she have that kind of arrangement with many other men?"

"Oh, indeed, yes. At least four besides Bobby. The house was hers, left to her by her late husband, Earl. She figured she needed at least two thousand dollars a month. She had a part-time job at the Blueberry Café where she made about three hundred a week. So she supplemented that with what she made from these five gentlemen friends, each paying between one and two hundred dollars a month. She must have pulled in another seven hundred. I can't tell you all their names, but I know she had a diary in which she had their names and telephone numbers, so she could keep track of who was coming and when. It was a very convenient arrangement for everybody." She paused a moment in abstracted thought. "She was a terribly attractive woman: pretty, but above all with a very attractive, happy, bubbly personality. You couldn't help loving her."

I thought of the tragic, grotesque figure next door, goggling at the ceiling, soaked in her own blood.

"So, what happened today, Mrs. Brown?"

Her skin became pasty, and she averted her eyes toward her French doors and the gray light outside. She gave a small sigh through her nose.

"Today . . . We were supposed to have coffee this morning, at eleven. She didn't show. She was usually punctual and usually showed up when we made arrangements, but you know how it is with bubbly people, sometimes they get involved in things and they forget, especially if you happen to be an old woman. However, Claire and I did meet three or four times a week for coffee, usually here, and she usually showed up. We had fun gossiping and chatting."

She paused, and I saw the glisten of tears in her eyes, and the small muscle in her jaw jumping. After a moment she took a deep breath and continued.

"This morning she didn't show, and to be honest I thought nothing of it. At about twelve noon I did notice a man leaving. I am not sure I would be able to describe him. I saw him from the back, and he was very average. Perhaps a little below six foot, neither fat nor thin, jeans, I think, or chinos, and a jacket which may have been some kind of anorak. It was green or blue, at that end of the color spectrum. It wasn't red or yellow or anything like that. I simply chalked it down as the reason why she hadn't turned up and thought nothing more of it, until this afternoon, shortly after four.

"I was just settling down to read a book, *Murder on the Golf Links*, not one of her best, when I heard this unearthly noise, like the wailing of a host of banshees. It made my skin go cold and the hair on the back of my neck stand up. I ran to the window and I saw poor Benny practically fall down the steps into the yard. He was screaming and pulling at his hair and staggering around in circles. Well, I rushed out to see what was the matter with the poor man and I couldn't believe it. He said, 'Call the cops, Edna! Call the cops! Claire's been hurt. She's been hurt real bad! I think she's dead!' I'll never forget those words as long as I live."

I nodded and glanced at the bow window a moment, thinking back to what Benny had said. "Mrs. Brown, think carefully. When your nondescript visitor left this morning, did you notice if he got into a car?"

"Yes." She nodded. "Now that you mention it, he got into a white Ford SUV. It was parked across the road, down a bit toward the church."

I exchanged a glance with Dehan. "How about this afternoon, when you went out to talk to Benny, did you notice anything or anyone unusual?"

She took a deep breath and puffed out her cheeks. "I would *really* not like to say. I was not paying attention to anything, and I might invent something that didn't really happen. You know how unreliable memory can be. The SUV might have been there again, but equally it might not."

"We are nearly done, Mrs. Brown. I have just one last question. Did Claire ever mention anyone, perhaps one of her clients or anybody else, who threatened her, or made her feel threatened or afraid? Did she ever mention being followed, stalked . . ." I spread my hands. "Anything of that sort?"

She became very serious, biting her top lip, lost in thought for a moment. Then she frowned.

"There was someone. It was a couple of months ago. A man who had heard from a friend of a friend of a friend, you know how it goes, that Claire had this arrangement with Benny and a few others. This character wanted in. She agreed to meet him, but she didn't like him and she told him no. I remember she told me he scared her. She said he came on too strong. She said he had violent eyes, and that phrase stuck in my mind. He came to the house. I don't know how he got her address, must have been from one of the boys, but he came around and threatened her. She threatened him right back, she was like that. She threatened him with the police and she told him she had friends who would take care of her. He went away and didn't come back."

Dehan asked, "That was a couple of months ago?"

"Yes, six or eight weeks, more or less."

"Did she get a name?"

"Yes . . ." She sighed again, searching her memory. "It was an odd name, he may have been French. I know he was foreign. Napoleon? Are Frenchmen really called Napoleon? I'm sorry I can't be more helpful. It was something like that."

"Don't worry." I stood, and Dehan stood with me. "One of the boys will know. Thank you for your help, Mrs. Brown."

She stood too and clenched her hands in front of her. Her face twisted suddenly with anxiety.

"What will become of her son?"

Dehan stated matter-of-factly, "She had a son."

"Oscar. He's sixteen. This will destroy him."

"Where is he?"

"When she had guests he stayed with a friend of hers, Begonia. I have the number . . ."

Dehan made the call to social services and then to Begonia. Arrangements were made to pick the boy up and take him into care and assign him a caseworker, and fifteen minutes later Edna Brown led us to the door and let us out into the cold night. Claire's body, now empty and beyond pain, camouflaged within a body bag, was being loaded into the back of an ambulance whose red-and-white lights pulsed a bleak, silent dirge against the side of the church. There was a chill, metallic rattle as the gurney folded its legs, and the body was swallowed by the black maw of the vehicle. Then suddenly Claire was gone. Absently, half in a trance, I found myself reciting:

"'Fear no more the lightning flash, nor the all-dreaded thunder stone; fear not slander, censure rash; thou hast finished joy and moan: all lovers young, all lovers must, consign to thee, and come to dust.'"

Dehan watched the doors of the ambulance slam closed and the guys climb aboard. Then it pulled away, toward Castle Hill Avenue, its siren wailing like it was on an urgent mission to save a life.

"What was that?" she asked and shuddered.

"Shakespeare, 'Fear no more the heat o' the sun,' from *Cymbeline*."

"It's sad."

I made the noise of thinking then sighed. "The final verse is happier. It's an incantation to protect the grave and the departed soul. 'No exorciser harm thee! Nor no witchcraft charm thee! Ghost unlaid forbear thee! Nothing ill come near thee! Quiet consummation have; and renowned be thy name!'"

She blinked at me a few times. Her mouth smiled but her eyes were having no part of it. "She could have done with a bit of that before she got murdered."

"No argument there, Dehan. No argument there. Come on, let's go see the chief."

We made our way in silence to the burgundy beast, and I slipped behind the wheel. The big cat roared, and I pulled away, back toward the 43rd. The streetlamps passed in a steady procession. I glanced at Dehan, silent beside me, and the light from the lamps and the passing, illuminated shop fronts bathed her face with alternating light and shadow.

She spoke suddenly, without looking at me. "So Mommy's Boy is back. What do you think, he's been away, killing somewhere else, and now he's back in town? Or he went into a kind of psychotic remission and now the urge is back?"

I thought about it for a moment, seeing the bed, soaked in brilliant red blood, and Claire's ghastly face gaping at the ceiling.

"I think it's too soon to say. We need to go through the old cases, and if possible talk to Alvarez, see what he remembers, what feelings he had. We also need to hear what Joe has to say about the makeup."

"Sure, but the lavender oil, and the sequence of the cuts, only a handful of people knew that."

I nodded once. "That much is true."

"So it has to be him."

"Maybe. Let's gather information first before we come to any conclusions."

"You think I'm jumping to conclusions?"

She still didn't look at me. I waited a moment and shook my head.

"No. There was a hell of a lot of information there. Too much to process straightaway. Some of it we haven't got yet. We need time to collate it, sift through it, and see what makes sense and what doesn't."

I glanced at her. She was still staring out of the windshield, but by the dim glow of the passing lights I could see there were tears on her cheeks. I didn't say anything. I reached over and held her hand with mine. She squeezed it, and we made the rest of the short journey in silence.

CHAPTER 3

INSPECTOR JOHN NEWMAN WATCHED US SIT DOWN, chewing his lip, and when we were comfortable lowered himself into his own chair.

"You will both have gathered why I want you to take lead on this case."

Dehan answered. "Yes, sir. It appears to be the Mommy's Boy killer, which became a cold case about five years back, when the killings stopped abruptly."

He observed her a moment from under his brows, then turned to me. "It stuck in my craw when that case went cold. Even if you weren't working the cold cases, I want you on that bastard's tail. I want you to hound him, sniff him out, and nail him to the wall. I am only sorry we have abolished the death penalty, John, because, may God forgive me, creatures like that do not deserve to live. I'm sorry, forgive me for expressing myself so frankly, Carmen. John, you are the best detective at the Forty-Third, and Carmen, you come a damned close second. I want you to find this son of a bitch, and I want you to eliminate him."

He held my gaze, and it was like the sheer power of his will was holding me, driving me to understand what he was communicating with his eyes, because the words were forbidden. The moment became surreal as it dawned on me what he was asking me to do. I scowled at him.

"Sir?"

He leaned forward with his elbows on his desk. The mild, amiable facade was gone. His eyes were hard, ruthless, and his mouth was an unrelenting line. The Bronx kid who'd fought his way up through the ranks before quotas and positive discrimination glared back at me and snarled.

"John, what he does to those women, he does while they are alive. They bleed out, but before they bleed out they go into shock from the sheer, unendurable horror of what he is doing to them. These are good, decent women struggling to raise their kids in a society that does not care about them. And this *bastard* breaks into their homes and visits pain and horror on them that we cannot even conceive; we cannot begin to *imagine*! And do you know what will happen when you arrest him and bring him to justice?"

"Sir, I am not sure I am following . . ."

"He will be prosecuted and he will be convicted because you are both damned good cops. And when he gets to Southport or Attica, he will then be *protected* from the other inmates by the prison staff. He will be urged to educate himself, better himself, he will see a psychologist and be encouraged to take up watercoloring, or creative writing. Maybe he'll even write his autobiography and become a millionaire!"

The silence that followed seemed to ring against the walls.

"Sir." I hesitated for just a moment. "Is there a personal issue here? I have to ask, because if there is . . ."

He shook his head. "No. There is no personal issue here, John. I was briefly involved in the original investigation. I saw firsthand what he did to the first two victims, how he killed them, and I watched how Detective Alvarez, who was a damned good cop, don't get me wrong, but I watched how he danced to this bastard's tune while woman after woman was tortured to death by this . . . *monster!* Alvarez never stood a chance. This bastard played him like a violin. What we need here is for you, both of you, to get inside his skin, get inside his mind"—he stabbed at his head with his finger—"and get a step ahead of him. He cannot be allowed to kill again—*ever!* Find him, John, and *stop* him!"

I hesitated again. "Sir, when you say stop him. We will find him and arrest . . ."

Dehan interrupted me. "We have the file, sir. We're going to take it home and go through it with a fine-tooth comb. We'll get inside his skin, and we will stop him, sir."

He stared at her awhile, then smiled and nodded. "I believe you will. I believe you will, Carmen."

We made our way down the stairs to the detectives' room. We now had a couple of steel filing cabinets for the cold cases, which had replaced the cartons we had started out with, and we worked our way through the approximate alphabetical order until we found the Mommy's Boy case. It was thick and detailed. We shared out the contents and started to read.

After a while, Dehan went and got two paper cups of coffee-like liquid. When she returned, she placed one in front of me, dropped into her chair, and crossed her boots on the corner of her desk. Then she started to talk as she leafed through the pages.

"There were five victims, Claire Carter makes six. The first was on the first of January, 2014. Mary Campbell, black, forty-five years old, murdered in her home in her bedroom. She was a single mother and had one son who was not at home at the time. Testimony from friends said that she was not a professional prostitute, but did see men and took money from them."

She tossed me some photographs. Some were of the crime scene and were strikingly similar to the scene we had just come from, the only difference being that Claire had been white, and Mary Campbell had been African American. There were a couple more photographs where she was smiling into the camera. She was slightly overweight, attractive, and seemed to smile easily.

Dehan was talking again. "The second, on the fifth of May,

2014, Maria Ortiz, Puerto Rican, thirty-eight years old, mother of four, one boy and three girls, murdered at home in her bedroom while the kids were staying with their aunt. She was a widow. Again, she saw men and received money, but did not have a pimp and didn't walk the streets."

She tossed over another set of photographs. I clipped the first lot together with a makeshift label and looked at Maria Ortiz. She was pretty, with a bright smile, slightly overweight. The crime scene was again identical in all significant details, except that Maria was Latina, neither black nor Caucasian. I clipped the pictures together and labeled them.

Dehan moved on. "Third, Olga Hernandez, hazard a wild guess at the date."

I glanced at the first two, studied her face a moment, and said, "Tenth of October?"

"Give the man a peanut. She was Colombian, forty-eight years old, and the single mother of one boy. Like the others, she was a dilettante lady of the night."

The pictures seemed to conform to the emerging pattern. She was slightly overweight, pretty, smiling, suggesting a sunny disposition. The crime scene was, at a glance, the same. I labeled them as I listened to Dehan.

"So we have one Afro-American, two Latinas, and now Sharon Lipschitz, Jewish, a nurse, mother of three boys and one girl, murdered, like the others, in her bedroom, while her husband was at work and the kids were at school. Friends were adamant that she was a respectable, faithful housewife. Unthinkable that she might be on the game. Take a shot at the date, Stone."

"Third of March, 2015. Every five months."

I examined the pictures. Sharon was pretty, like the others. The photographs showed her laughing, smiling, bright. The crime scene was as the others.

Dehan sighed. "Finally, Margaret Allen, white, divorced mother of one boy and one girl. No known connection with prostitution, dilettante or otherwise. Murdered, like the others, in her bedroom, while the kids were at school. Take a shot at the date."

She looked up and raised an eyebrow. I drew breath but stopped short. "Not the eighth of August 2015."

She shook her head. "Third of January."

"Son of a bitch."

She tossed me the pictures. Again, she was bright, pretty, laughing, and the crime scene was identical. I clipped them and labeled them while I spoke.

"He knows the cops are going to look for patterns of behavior to try and profile him, so he creates patterns and then breaks them. Dates, kids, race, prostitution, sexual morality—he doesn't give a damn about any of it."

Dehan was nodding slowly. "The only constants are that the women are slightly overweight, and, from witness statements and the photographs, they all seem to have been happy, lively, and friendly."

"Possibly a soft touch for a predator. But here's the brilliant part of his strategy: we don't know if these are constants at all. They are simply what has remained constant so far."

She banged her fist gently on the desk. "So is Claire Carter part of this strategy? Or has he just been away killing out of state, with a completely different MO?"

"We don't know." I sat forward and laid both hands on the desk. "That, Dehan, is the first thing that we need to get to grips with. He is smart, and what we know about him is practically zero. This is what the chief was talking about. He played Alvarez like a violin. Had him chasing a profile that was all smoke and mirrors and did not actually exist."

"Jesus . . . !"

"We need to set up a board where we can build profiles of the victims and of suspects, and we are going to need a team to do the donkey work. But first we are going to need to take this home and digest it. Because there is one thing we *can* be sure of. All this misdirection and smoke and mirrors is designed to conceal something. And that something is there to be concealed. Note: one, he kills women, and all the elaborate trickery is *for the purpose* of enabling him to kill women. Two, he cuts off the left breast so that the victim bleeds to death. The left breast is over the heart, the source of life and love. This, you can stake my career and my reputation on it, is as central to his urge to kill as is killing women. All the rest of it may be show, but the need to kill women and remove their left breast, those are central and integral to his homicidal drive."

She nodded a lot. Then raised her right hand with her index finger erect, while still nodding. "And there is one more thing, Stone. It doesn't stand out, it's actually almost buried under all the other details. Every one of the victims has had at least one son."

I thought about it. "Yeah, I am no psychologist, as you once pointed out to me, but two gets you twenty that in his mind the boy—the victim's son—represents him; *is* him."

"Yeah, you're probably right. We need to get an FBI profiler in and get some idea about who we're chasing here."

"Agreed."

We sat in silence awhile, looking at each other. She seemed suddenly small and very vulnerable. I smiled at her.

"You've never been on one of these before?"

She shook her head. "No."

"It's harrowing, and it never gets any easier. But"—I shrugged —"you build up defenses. You learn to deal with it somehow."

"I need a drink."

"Okay, let's get this stuff home. We'll order in pizza and a bottle of wine."

"Pizza?" She screwed up her face. "I'll try, but I might just stick to tequila." She swung her feet off the desk and sat forward. "Did Alvarez have anyone in his sights? Was there *anyone* of interest?"

"Yeah." I stood and pulled my coat off the back of my chair, then picked up the file and leafed through it. "James Campbell . . ."

She frowned. "Campbell? Any relation to the first victim?"

"Mary Campbell, yeah, her son. Alvarez's notes say he is a minister in a religious mission on Castle Hill and Homer. He says he displays signs of being seriously misogynistic and perhaps a religious fanatic. However, he was unable to link him to the other murders and never had enough to try and get a psych evaluation."

She leaned back. "He's got to be worth a visit. The first victim's son, and all the victims have sons . . . ?"

I nodded and kept reading. "There was also a Nelson Vargas, known to be a member of the Cabras gang. Rap sheet as long as your arm, but no serious charges made to stick, suspected of several murders, mostly gang related, rape, dealing . . ." I shook my head as I read. "You name it."

"How's he connected to this?"

"Maria Ortiz called the cops five days before she was killed and complained that he had threatened her with rape and murder. Ring a bell?"

I glanced at her. She said, "Claire made the same complaint. We need to find out if it's the same guy. Anyone else come on Alvarez's radar?"

"Yeah, he had no trouble finding suspects, just making it stick. George Allen, Margaret Allen's ex-husband. That's the last victim before he went off the radar."

"That's odd." I looked at her. She was frowning. "It just feels wrong. You'd expect her to be the first. He kills her and gets a taste for it. Not to start killing strangers and then kill his own wife. It feels wrong."

I made a "what can I tell you?" face and read on.

"He's the sales director of SuperWare, a company that develops and produces supermarket software."

"Supermarket software?"

"Sales director. You don't need to be a genius, but you do need to be smart and a strategist. He moved to Rochester five years ago, shortly before the killings stopped."

She grunted, and I turned a page.

"Last one, Golam Heitz."

"Golam Heitz? Are you kidding me?"

"Nope, and get this, he was an orderly at the same hospital where Sharon Lipschitz was a nurse, the St. Barnabas, Third Avenue, in West Bronx, near the zoo. Alvarez didn't like him. His notes have him as, and I quote, 'Neurotic nerd, arrogant, spotty, thinks he's a genius, could use a bath.'" I closed the folder. "That's it. No other suspects showed up, and the main problem, according to his notes, was connecting any one of the suspects to all the murders. They are all more or less loosely connected to at least *one* of the murders, but none is linked, however tenuously, to *all* of them."

She nodded, sniffed, and sat looking around the room, now largely empty and partially dark. I pulled on my coat, but she didn't move. She said, "None is, that's correct, right? Not 'none are'?"

"Yes, Dehan, 'none is' is correct. Shall we go?"

She sighed and stood and pulled on her jacket. "I guess it used to have an apostrophe, right?"

We crossed the room and headed out into the frosty night. The billows of condensation from her breath glowed in the lamplight, and across the road a layer of white frost lay across the roof of my ancient Jaguar. She looked up at me and blinked, and I was possessed by a powerful need to protect her and care for her. She said:

"After the first 'n': 'n' apostrophe, 'one.'"

I frowned. "What?"

"Not one is, 'n' apostrophe 'one' is, 'none is.' Right?"

I laughed. "You're nuts."

"Take me somewhere you can hug me that the cops won't see us."

We made our way carefully down the steps and across the slippery blacktop toward my car, and home.

Scan the QR code below to purchase MOMMY'S LITTLE KILLER.
Or go to: righthouse.com/mommys-little-killer

Made in the USA
Coppell, TX
09 February 2025

45683326R00121